FOOL'S GOLD?

To avoid a scene like the one recently played in the war room, Rolf Emerson decided it was best to inform Leonard of the new arrangements he'd made for the alien pilot, who had given his name as Zor.

Zor!—the name mentioned in debriefing sessions following the rescue at the Macross mounds. It had seemed coincidental then, but now...

Zor!

A notorious name these past fifteen years; a name whispered by everyone connected with Robotechnology; a name at once despised and held in the greatest reverence. Zor, whom the Zentraedi had credited with the discovery of Protoculture; Zor, the Tirolian scientist who had sent the SDF-1 to Earth, unwittingly causing the near destruction of the planet and the eclipse of the Human race.

Of course it was possible that Zor was a common name among these people called the Masters. But then again...

The ROBOTECH™ Series
Published by Ballantine Books:

ROBOTECH™ #8

METAL FIRE

Jack McKinney

A Del Rey Book

BALLANTINE BOOKS • NEW YORK

A Del Rey Book
Published by Ballantine Books

Library of Congress Catalog Card Number: 87-91146

ISBN 0-345-34141-4

Printed in Canada

First Edition: August 1987

Cover Art by David Schleinkofer

FOR REBA WEST, JONATHEN ALEXANDER,
TONY OLIVER, AND THE DOZEN OTHERS
WHOSE VOICES BROUGHT THESE
CHARACTERS TO LIFE.

CHAPTER
ONE

> *EXEDORE: So, Admiral, there is little doubt: [Zentraedi and Human] genetic makeup points directly at a common point of origin.*
> *ADMIRAL GLOVAL: Incredible.*
> *EXEDORE: Isn't it. Furthermore, while examining the data we noticed many common traits, including a penchant on the part of both races to indulge in warfare. . . . Yes, both races seem to enjoy making war.*
>
> From Exedore's intel reports to the SDF-2 High Command

ONCE BEFORE, AN ALIEN FORTRESS HAD CRASHED on Earth . . .

Its arrival had put an end to almost ten years of global civil war; and its resurrection had ushered in armageddon. That fortress's blackened, irradiated remains lay buried under a mountain of earth, heaped upon it by the very men and women who had rebuilt the ship on what would have been its island grave. But unbeknownst to those who mourned its loss, the soul of that great ship had survived the body and inhabited it still—an entity living in the shadows of the technology it animated, waiting to be freed by its natural keepers, and until then haunting the world chosen for its sorry exile. . . .

This new fortress, this most recent gift from heaven's more sinister side, had announced its arrival, not with tidal and tectonic upheavals, but with open warfare and devastation—death's bloodstained calling cards. Nor was this fortress derelict and uncontrolled in its fateful fall but

1

driven, brought down to Earth by the unwilling minor players in its dark drama. . . .

"ATAC Fifteen to air group!" Dana Sterling yelled into her mike over the din of battle. "Hit 'em again with everything you have! Try to keep their heads down! They're throwing everything but old shoes at us down here!"

Less than twenty-four hours ago her team, the 15th squad, Alpha Tactical Armored Corps, had felled this giant, not with sling and shot, but with a coordinated strike launched at the fortress's Achilles' heel—the core reactor governing the ship's bio-gravitic network. It had dropped parabolically from geosynchronous orbit, crash-landing in the rugged hills several kilometers distant from Monument City.

Hardly a *coincidental* impact point, Dana said to herself as she bracketed the fortress in the sights of the Hovertank's rifle/cannon.

The 15th, in Battloid mode, was moving across a battle zone that was like some geyser field of orange explosions and high-flung dirt and rock—a little like a cross between a moonscape and the inside of Vesuvius on a busy day.

Up above, the TASC fighters, the Black Lions among them, roared in for another pass. The glassy green tear-drop-cannon of the fortress didn't seem as effective in atmosphere, and so far there had been no sign of the snowflake-shields. But the enemy's hull, rearing above the assaulting Battloids, still seemed able to soak up all the punishment they could deal it and stand unaltered.

An elongated hexagon, angular and relatively flat, the alien fortress measured over five miles in length, half that in width. Its thickly plated hull was the same lackluster gray of the Zentraedi ships used in the First Robotech War; but in contrast to those organic leviathan dread-naughts, the fortress boasted a topography to rival that of a cityscape. Along the long axis of its dorsal surface was a mile-long raised portion of superstructure that resembled the peaked roofs of many twentieth-century houses. Forward was a concentrically coiled conelike projection Louie Nichols had christened "a Robotech teat"; aft were massive Reflex thruster ports; and elsewhere, weapons stations, deep crevices, huge louvered panels, ziggurats, onions domes, towers like two-tined forks, stairways and bridges, armored docking bays, and the articulated muzzles of the ship's countless segmented "insect leg" cannons.

Below the sawtooth ridge the pilots of the fortress had chosen as their crash site was Monument City, and several miles distant across two slightly higher ridges, the remains of New Macross and the three Human-made mounds that marked the final resting place of the super dimensional fortresses.

Dana wondered if the SDF-1 had something to do with this latest warfare. If these invaders were indeed the Robotech Masters (and not some other band of XT galactic marauders), had they come to avenge the Zentraedi in some way? Or worse still—as many were asking—was Earth fighting a new war with micronized Zentraedi?

Child of a Human father and a Zentraedi mother—the only known child of such a marriage—Dana had good reason to disprove this latter hypothesis.

That *some* of the invaders were humanoid was a fact only recently accepted by the High Command. Scarcely a month ago Dana had been face-to-face with a pilot of one of the invaders' bipedal mecha—the so-called Bioroids. Bowie Grant had been even closer, but Dana was the one who had yet to get over the encounter. All at once the war had personalized itself; it was no longer machine against machine, Hovertank against Bioroid.

Not that that mattered in the least to the hardened leaders of the UEG. Since the end of the First Robotech War, Human civilization had been on a downhill slide;

and if it hadn't come to Humans facing aliens, it probably would have been Humans against Humans.

Dana heard a sonic roar through the Hovertank's external pickups and looked up into a sky full of new generation Alpha fighters, snub-nosed descendants of the Veritechs.

The place was dense with smoke and flying fragments from missile bursts, and the missile's retwisting tracks. As Dana watched, one pair of VTs finished a pass only to have two alien assault ships lift into the air and go up after them. Dana yelled a warning over the Forward Air Control net, then switched from the FAC frequency to her own tactical net because the real showdown had begun; two blue Bioroids had popped up from behind boulders near the fortress.

The blues opened fire and the ATACs returned it with interest; the range was medium-long, but energy bolts and annihilation discs skewed and splashed furiously, searching for targets. At Dana's request, a Tactical Air Force fighter-bomber flight came in to drop a few dozen tons of conventional ordnance while the TASCs got set up for their next run.

Abruptly, a green-blue light shone from the fortress, and a half second later it lay under a hemisphere of spindriftlike stuff, a dome of radiant cobweb, and all incoming beams and solids were splashing harmlessly from it.

But the enemy could fire through their own shield, and did, knocking down two of the retreating bombers and two approaching VTs with cannonfire. Whatever the damage to the bio-gravitic system was, it plainly hadn"t robbed the fortress of all its stupendous power.

Dana's hand went out for the mode selector lever. She attuned her thoughts to the mecha and threw the lever to G, reconfiguring from Battloid to Gladiator. The Hovertank was now a squat, two-legged SPG (self-propelled gun), with a single cannon stretching out in front of it.

Nearby, in the scant cover provided by hillside granite outcroppings and dislodged boulders, the rest of the 15th —Louie Nichols, Bowie Grant, Sean Phillips, and Sergeant Angelo Dante among others—similarly reconfigured, was unleashing salvos against the stationary fortress.

"Man, these guys are tough as nails!" Dana heard Sean say over the net. "They aren't budging an inch!"

And they aren't likely to, Dana knew. *We're fighting for our home; they're fighting for their ship and their only hope of survival.*

"At this rate the fighting could go on forever," Angelo said. "Somebody better think of something quick." And everyone knew he wasn't talking about sergeants, lieutenants, or anybody else who might be accused of working for a living; the brass better realize it was making a mistake, or come evening they would need at least one new Hovertank squad.

Then Angelo picked up on a blue that had charged from behind a rock and was headed straight for Bowie's *Diddy-Wa-Diddy.* The attitude and posture of Bowie's mecha suggested that it was distracted, unfocused.

Damn kid, woolgathering! "Look out, Bowie!"

But then Sean appeared in Battloid mode, firing with the rifle/cannon, the blue stumbling as it broke up in the blazing beams, then going down.

"Wake up and stay on your toes, Bowie," Angelo growled. "That's the third time today ya fouled up."

"Sorry," Bowie returned. "Thanks, Sarge."

Dana was helping Louie Nichols and another trooper try to drive back blues who were crawling forward from cover to cover on their bellies, the first time the Bioroids had ever been seen to do such a thing.

"These guys just won't take no for an answer," Dana grated, raking her fire back and forth at them.

* * *

Remote cameras positioned along the battle perimeter brought the action home to headquarters. An intermittent beeping sound (like nonsense Morse) and horizontal noise bars disrupted the video transmission. Still, the picture was clear: the Tactical Armored units were taking a beating.

Colonel Rochelle vented his frustration in a slow exhale of smoke, and stubbed out his cigarette in the already crowded ashtray. There were three other staff officers with him at the long table, at the head of which sat Major General Rolf Emerson.

"The enemy is showing no sign of surrender," Rochelle said after a moment. "And the Fifteenth is tiring fast."

"Hit them harder," Colonel Rudolph suggested. "We've got the air wing commander standing by. A surgical strike—nuclear, if we have to."

Rochelle wondered how the man had ever reached his current rank. "I won't even address that suggestion. We have no clear-cut understanding of that ship's energy shield. And what if the cards don't fall our way? Earth would be finished."

Rudolph blinked nervously behind his thick glasses. "I don't see that the threat would be any greater than the attacks already launched against Monument."

Butler, the staff officer seated opposite Rudolph spoke to that. "This isn't *The War of the Worlds*, Colonel—at least not yet. We don't even know what they want from us."

"Do I have to remind you gentlemen about the attack on Macross Island?" Rudolph's voice took on a harder edge. "Twenty years ago isn't exactly ancient history, is it? If we're going to wait for an *explanation*, we might as well surrender right now."

Rochelle was nodding his head and lighting up another

cigarette. "I'm against escalation at this point," he said, smoke and breath drawn in.

Rolf Emerson, gloved hands folded in front of him on the table, sat silently, taking in his staff's assessments and opinions but saying very little. If it were left up to him to decide, he would attempt to open up a dialogue with the unseen invaders. True, the aliens had struck the first blow, but it had been the Earth Forces who had been goading them into continued strikes ever since. Unfortunately, though, he was not the one chosen to decide things; he had to count on Commander Leonard for that . . . *And may heaven help us,* he thought.

"We just can't let them *sit* there!" Rudolph was insisting.

Emerson cleared his voice, loud enough to cut through the separate conversations that were in progress, and the table fell silent. The audio monitors brought the noise of battle to them once again; in concert, permaplas windowpanes rattled to the sounds of distant explosions.

"This battle requires more than just hardware and manpower, gentlemen. . . . We'll give them back the ground we've taken because it's of no use to us right now. We'll withdraw our forces temporarily, until we have a workable plan."

The 15th acknowledged the orders to pull back and ceased fire. Other units were reporting heavy casualties, but their team had been fortunate: seven dead, three wounded—counts that would have been judged insignificant twenty years ago, when Earth's population was more than just a handful of hardened survivors.

Emerson dismissed his staff, returned to his office, and requested to meet with the supreme commander. But Leonard surprised him by telling him to stay put, and five minutes later burst through the door like an angry bull.

"There's got to be some way to crack open that ship!"

Leonard railed. "I will not accept defeat! I will not accept the status quo!"

Emerson wondered if Leonard would have accepted the status quo if he had sweated out the morning in the seat of a Hovertank, or a Veritech.

The supreme commander was every bit Emerson's opposite in appearance as well as temperament. He was a massive man, tall, thick-necked, and barrel-chested, with a huge, hairless head, and heavy jowls that concealed what had once been strong, angular features, Prussian features, perhaps. His standard uniform consisted of white britches, black leather boots, and a brown longcoat fringed at the shoulders. But central to this ensemble was an enormous brass belt buckle, which seemed to symbolize the man's foursquare materialistic solidity.

Emerson, on the other hand, had a handsome face with a strong jaw, thick eyebrows, long and well drawn like gulls' wings, and dark, sensitive eyes, more close-set than they should have been, somewhat diminishing an otherwise intelligent aspect.

Leonard commenced pacing the room, his arms folded across his chest, while Emerson remained seated at his desk. Behind him was a wallscreen covered with schematic displays of troop deployment.

"Perhaps Rudolph's plan," Leonard mused.

"I strongly oppose it, Comman—"

"You're too cautious, Emerson," Leonard interrupted. "Too cautious for your own good."

"We had no choice, Commander. Our losses—"

"Don't talk to me of *losses*, man! We can't let these aliens run roughshod over us! I propose we adopt Rudolph's strategy. A surgical strike is our only recourse."

Emerson thought about objecting, but Leonard had swung around and slammed his hands flat on the table, silencing him almost before he began.

"I will not tolerate any delays!" the commander warned him, bulldog jowls shaking. "If Rudolph's plan doesn't meet with your approval, then come up with a better one!"

Emerson stifled a retort and averted his eyes. For an instant, the commander's shaved head inches from his own, he understood why Leonard was known to some as Little Dolza.

"Certainly, Commander," he said obediently. "I understand." What Emerson understood was that Chairman Moran and the rest of the UEG council were beginning to question Leonard's fitness to command, and Leonard was feeling the screws turn.

Leonard's cold gaze remained in place. "Good," he said, certain he had made himself clear. "Because I want an end to all this madness and I'm holding *you* responsible.... After all," he added, turning and walking away, "you're supposed to be the miracle man."

The 15th had a clear view of the jagged ridgeline and downed fortress from their twelfth-story quarters in the barracks compound. Between the compound and twin peaks that dominated the view, the land was lifeless and incurably rugged, cratered from the countless Zentraedi death bolts rained upon it almost twenty years before.

The barracks' ready-room was posh by any current standards: spacious, well-lit, equipped with features more befitting a recreation room, including video games and a bar. Most of the squad was done in, already in the sack or on their way, save for Dana Sterling, too wired for sleep, Angelo Dante, who had little use for it on any occasion, and Sean Phillips, who was more than accustomed to long hours.

The sergeant couldn't tear himself away from the view and seemed itching to get back into battle.

"We should still be out there fighting—am I right or am I right?" Angelo pronounced, directing his words to Sean only because he was seated nearby. "We'll be fighting this war when our pensions come due unless we defeat those monsters with one big shot; the whistle blows and everybody goes."

At twenty-six, the sergeant was the oldest member of the 15th, also the tallest, loudest, and deadliest—as sergeants are wont to be. He had met his match for impulsiveness in Dana, and recklessness in Sean, but the final results had yet to be tallied.

Sean, chin resting on his hand, had his back turned to the windows and to Angie. Long-haired would-be Casanova of the 15th and of nearly every other outfit in the barracks compound, he fancied conquests of a softer sort. But at the moment he was too exhausted for campaigns of any class.

"The brass'll figure out what to do, Angie," he told the seargeant tiredly, still regarding himself as a lieutenant no matter what the brass thought of him. "Haven't you heard? They know everything. Personally, I'm tired."

Angelo stopped pacing, looking around to make sure Bowie wasn't there. "By the way, what's with Bowie?"

This seemed to bring Sean around some, but Angelo declined to follow his comment up with an explanation.

"Why? He got a problem? You should have said something during the debriefing."

The sergeant put his hands on his hips. "He's been screwing up. That's not a *problem* in combat; it's a major malfunction."

Some would have expected the presence of the fortress to have cast a pall over the city, but that was not the case. In fact, in scarcely a week's time the often silent ship (except when stirred up by the armies of the Southern Cross) had become an accepted feature of the landscape, and something of an object of fascination. Had the area of the crash site not been cordoned off, it's likely that half of Monument would have streamed up into the hills in hopes of catching a glimpse of the thing. As it was, business went on as usual. But historians and commentators were quick to offer explanations, pointing to the behavior of the populace of besieged cities of the past, Beirut of the last century, and countless others during the Global Civil War at the century's end.

Even Dana Sterling, and Nova Satori, the cool but alluring lieutenant with the Global Military Police, were not immune to the fortress's ominous enchantment. Even though they had both seen the deadlier side of its nature revealed.

Just now they shared a table in one of Monument's most popular cafés—a checkerboard-patterned tile floor, round tables of oak, and chairs of wrought iron—with a view of the fortress that surpassed the barracks' overlook.

Theirs had been less than a trouble-free relationship, but Dana had made a deal with herself to try to patch things up. Nova was agreeable and had an hour or so she could spare.

They were in their uniforms, their techno-hairbands in place, and as such the two women looked like a pair of military bookends: Dana, short and lithe, with a globe of swirling blond hair; and taller Nova, with her polished face and thick fall of black hair.

But they were hardly of a mind about things.

"I have lots of dreams," Dana was saying, "the waking kind and the sleeping kind. Sometimes I dream about meeting a man and flying to the edge of the universe with him—"

She caught herself abruptly. How in the world had she gotten onto this subject? She had started off by apologizing, explaining the pressures she had been under. Then somehow she had considered confiding to Nova about the disturbing images and trances concerning the red Bioroid pilot, the one called Zor, not certain whether the MP lieutenant would feel duty-bound to report the matter.

Maybe it had something to do with looking at the fortress and knowing the red Bioroid was out there somewhere? And then all of a sudden she was babbling about her childhood fantasies and Nova was studying her with a get-the-strait-jacket look.

"Don't you think it's time you grew up?" said Nova. "Took life a little more seriously?"

Dana turned to her, the spell broken. "Listen, I'm as attentive to duty as the next person! I didn't get my commission just because of who my parents are, so don't patronize me—huh?"

She jumped to her feet. A big MP had just come in with Bowie, looking hangdog, traipsing behind. The MP saluted Nova and explained.

"We caught him in an off-limits joint, ma'am. He has a valid pass, but what shall we do with him?"

"Not a word, Dana!" Nova cautioned. Then she asked the MP, "Which off-limits place?"

"A bar over in the Gauntlet, ma'am."

"Wait a minute," said Bowie, hoping to save his neck. "It wasn't a bar, ma'am, it was a jazz club!" He looked back and forth between Nova and Dana, searching for the line of least resistance, realizing all the while that it was a fine line between bar and club. But being busted for drinking was going to cost him more points than straying into a restricted area. Maybe if he displayed the guilt they obviously expected him to feel . . .

"Where they have been known to roll soldiers who wake up bleeding in some alley!" Nova snapped. "If the army didn't need every ATAC right now, I'd let you think that over for a week in the lockup!"

Nova was forcing the harsh tone in her voice. What she actually felt was closer to amusement than anger. Any minute now Dana would try to intervene on Grant's behalf; and Grant was bound to foul up again, which would then reflect on Dana. Nova smiled inside: it felt so good to have the upper hand.

Bowie was stammering an explanation and apology, far from heartfelt, but somehow convincing. Nova, however, put a quick end to it and continued to read him the riot act.

"And furthermore, I fully appreciate the pressure you've all been under, but we can't afford to make allowances for *special cases*. Do you understand me, *Private*?!"

The implication was clear enough: Bowie was being warned that his relationship with General Emerson wouldn't be taken into account.

Dana was gazing coldly at Bowie, nodding along with the lieutenant's lecture, but at the same time she was managing to slip Bowie a knowing wink, as if to say: *Just agree with her.*

Bowie caught on at last. "I promise not to do it again, *sir!*"

Meanwhile Nova had turned to Dana. "If Lieutenant Sterling is willing to take responsibility for you and keep you out of trouble, I'll let this incident go. But next time I won't be so lenient."

Dana consented, her tone suggesting rough things ahead for Bowie Grant, and Nova dismissed her agent.

"Shall we finish our coffee?" Nova asked leadingly.

Dana thought carefully before responding. Nova was up to no good, but Dana suddenly saw a way to turn the incident to her own advantage. And Bowie's as well.

"I think it would be better if I started *proving* myself to you by taking care of my new responsibility," she said stiffly.

"Yes, you do that," Nova drawled, sounding like the Wicked Witch of the West.

Later, walking back to the barracks, Dana had some serious words with her charge.

"Nova's not playing around. Next time she'll probably feed you to the piranhas. Bowie, what's wrong? First you louse up in combat, then you go looking for trouble in town. And where'd you steal a valid pass, by the way?"

He shrugged, head hung. "I keep spares. Sorry, I

didn't mean to cause any friction between you and Nova. You're a good friend, Dana."

Dana smiled down at him. "Okay . . . But there's one thing you can do for me. . . ."

Bowie was waiting for her to finish, when Dana's open hand came around without warning and slapped him forcefully on the back—almost throwing him off his feet—and with it Dana's hearty: "Cheer up! Everything's going to be fine!"

CHAPTER
TWO

I wish someone would call time out,
They're welcome to disarm me,
We are the very model of
A modern techno army.

Bowie Grant, "With Apologies to Gilbert and Sullivan"

THIRTEEN, ROLF EMERSON SAID TO HIMSELF WHEN he had completed his count of the staff officers grouped around the briefing room's tables. The tables would have formed a triangle of sorts, save for the fact that Commander Leonard's desk (at what would have been the triangle's apex) was curved. This was also a bad sign. Ordinarily, Emerson was not a superstitious man, but recent developments in world events had begun to work a kind of atavism on him. And if Human consciousness was going to commence a backward slide, who was he to march against it?

"This meeting has been called to discuss strategic approaches we might employ against the enemy," the supreme commander announced when the last member of his staff had seated himself. "We must act quickly and decisively, gentlemen; so I expect you to keep your remarks brief and to the point." Leonard got to his feet, both hands flat on the table. His angry eyes found Rolf Emerson. "General . . . go ahead."

Emerson rose, hoping his plan would fly; it seemed the only rational option, but that didn't guarantee anything, with Chairman Moran holding Leonard's feet to the fire, and Leonard passing the courtesy along down the chain of command. *Brief and to the point*, he reminded himself.

"I propose we recommence an attack on the fortress . . . but only as a diversionary tactic. That ship remains an unknown quantity, and I think it's imperative we get a small scouting unit inside for a fast recon."

This set off a lot of talk about demolition teams, battlefield nukes, and the like.

Rolf raised his voice. "Gentlemen, the goal is not to destroy the fortress. We have to ascertain some measure of understanding of the aliens' purpose. Need I remind you that this ship is but one of many?"

Leonard quieted the table. Twice, Emerson had said *alien* as opposed to enemy, but he decided to address that some other time. Right now, the major general's plan sounded good. A bit risky, but logical, and he stated as much.

To everyone's surprise, Colonel Rudolph concurred. "After all, what do we know about the enemy?" he pointed out.

Leonard asked Rolf to address this.

"We have tentative evidence that they're Human or nearly Human in biogenetic terms," Emerson conceded. "But that might only apply to their warrior class. We *do* know that the Robotechnology we've seen them use is much more advanced than ours, and we have no idea what else they're capable of."

"All the more reason to recon that ship," Rudolph said after a moment.

There was general agreement, but Colonel Rochelle thought to ask whether a team really could penetrate the fortress, given the aliens' superior firepower and defenses.

"If it's the right team," Rolf answered him.

"And the Fifteenth is the one for the job," Commander Leonard said decisively.

Emerson contradicted warily: it was true that the 15th had had some remarkable successes lately, but it was still a relatively untested outfit, and there were some among the team who certainly weren't qualified for the job. . . .

But Leonard cut him off before he had a chance to name names, which was just as well.

"General Emerson, you know the Fifteenth is the best team for this job."

There was general agreement again, while Emerson hid his consternation. Dana and Bowie had entered the military because that was where they were needed, and a stint in the service was expected of all able-bodied young people. Emerson had encouraged Bowie to enter the academy, because Dana had already decided to and because Emerson was well aware that that was what Bowie's parents would have wanted.

It was just bad luck that a war had come along. Perhaps it would have been better for Emerson to renege on his promises to the Grants, to have let the kid go off and study music, play piano in nightspots . . . maybe that way Bowie might have been the last piano player cremated by an alien deathray, or might have survived while the rest of the Human race hurled itself onto the pyre of battle to stop the invaders.

But Emerson didn't think Bowie would see things that way. Bowie had seen the invaders at far closer range than Emerson, and Emerson had heard and seen enough to know that Earth was in a win-or-die war.

Still, the idea of putting the 15th out on the tip of the lance yet again went against Emerson's sense of justice and of military wisdom; this was a commando job, not a tank mission.

Commander Leonard was well aware of Emerson's relationship to Bowie Grant; but promises or no promises, Bowie was a soldier, end of story. Leonard wasn't spelling all this out for everyone in the room, but Rolf had picked up the commander's subliminal message.

Rudolph and Rochelle also understood Rolf's predicament, but they, too, were resolute in their decision: it had to be the 15th.

"I suggest we prepare an options list," Emerson told the staff, "a variety of plans and mixes for the forces involved."

Leonard seemed to consider that. He addressed Colonel Rudolph: "Get together with the ATACs' CO and hammer out one scenario using the Fifteenth." He ordered Rolf to get the G3 shop to begin assembling alternatives.

Emerson acknowledged the order, relieved. But as the meeting broke up, Leonard pulled Rudolph aside, waiting until Emerson was gone.

"Colonel, I'm directing you to present this mission to the Fifteenth ATAC and Lieutenant Sterling as an order, not a proposal. We can't waste time dawdling." *And I can't waste time arguing with my subordinates, nor can I risk Emerson's resigning just now. My neck's on the block!*

Rudolph snapped to smartly. "Sir!"

The commander continued in a confidential tone. "We must put aside Rolf's personal matters and get on with the war."

"What d'ya think—that I'd *volunteer* us for this mission?" Dana said to her squad after the orders had come down from Headquarters. "Somebody has to recon that fortress—"

"And we're that somebody," Sean finished for her. "HQ wants to know who it's fighting."

"They'll be fighting *me* if this keeps up," Sergeant

Dante threatened, clenching his big hands and adopting a boxer's stance.

The primaries of the 15th were grouped in their barracks ready-room, trying to find someone to blame for HQ's directive. Dana had already had it out with Colonel Rudolph, citing all the action the team had seen lately, their need for R & R, the sorry state of their ordnance and Hovertanks. But it all fell on deaf ears: when the supreme commander said jump, you jumped. With or without a chute.

"Hey, Sarge, I thought you *wanted* to keep fighting," Sean reminded him.

Dante glared at him. "I just don't like being used like a pawn in Leonard's game of 'name the alien.' We've gotta go out there and risk our lives to save their reputations."

"How *literary* of you, Angelo," Dana said sharply. "What the heck does *reputation* have to do with any of this?" She gestured out the window in the direction of the downed fortress. "That ship is at least a *potential* threat. What are we supposed to do—turn it into an amusement park ride?"

"How are we even going to get in?" Louie Nichols thought to ask.

The team turned to regard the whiz kid of the Southern Cross, waiting for him to suggest something. With his gaunt, angular face, top-heavy thatch of deep brown hair, and everpresent wraparound opaque goggles, Louie came closer to resembling an alien than Dana herself. Some members of Professor Cochran's group actually believed that Louie had patterned himself after the infamous Exedore, the Zentraedi Minister of Affairs during the Robotech War.

"It's difficult enough analyzing their technology. But getting *inside* their ship . . . How are we supposed to pull that off?"

Angelo looked at Louie in disbelief. "Get in? How are we gonna get out, Louie, how are we gonna get *out*?! I don't think you realize there's a chance we may not return from this mission alive."

Sean made a wry face. "Pity . . . she's gonna miss me when I'm gone."

At the same time, Louie exclaimed, "Gone?!" Bowie asked, "Isn't that a song?" and Dana said, "Knock it off."

Sean acknowledged the rebuke with a bemused smile. "You're right," he told Dana. "This mission is more important than my miss. What's it matter, right? We're tough."

"That's the right stuff," Dana enthused. "And there's no other way to pull this mission off but to, well, to just *do it*!"

The sergeant was nodding in agreement now, wondering where his earlier comments had come from. If Dana the halfbreed could get behind it, he could, too.

"All right," he said rallying to the cause. "We'll make them rue the day they touched down on this planet."

The 15th had a little over twelve hours to kill, and sleep was out of the question. Dana had her doubts about giving anybody permission to leave the barracks, but realized that keeping them cooped up would only give them time to ferment and perhaps explode. She issued "cinderella" passes—good until midnight—along with dire threats about what Nova's MPs would do to anybody who screwed up in town or came back late.

Sean left to visit a good friend who found prebattle good-byes aphrodisiac. Louie Nichols sat down to tinker with his helmet video transmitters. Angie nursed drinks and cigars in the dark privacy of his own quarters. And Bowie Grant insisted on treating Dana to the finest beers to be had in Monument City.

Twenty minutes later, Dana and Bowie were lifting frosted, conelike pilsner glasses of pale, foamy beer and clinking them together in a toast to better times.

Bowie contorted his face for a clownish look. "I figured it was the least I could do after what you did for me yesterday."

As Dana lowered her glass her hand brushed something that he had slid over to her.

"What's this?" It was a gorgeous little blossom of delicate red, hot pink, and coral, and tones in between. "A flower?"

"An orchid, Dana. For good luck."

She pinned it ceremonially onto her torso harness, near her heart. "You're sweet, Bowie. And maybe too sensitive for this line of work. What d'ya think?"

Bowie drew a deep breath. "Well, I prefer music to space warfare, if that's what you mean. You know this wasn't my idea."

Dana looked hard at her handsome friend, thinking back through years of peaceful and playful memories, back to when their parents were still on-world—when her memory of them was still alive. . . .

She debated for a moment, then it occurred to her—as it did more strongly with each action she fought in—that for her, Bowie, the 15th, the Human race, tomorrow might be the last, for any or all of them.

Bowie had been making mistakes lately in a very uncharacteristic way. Dana was no shrink and she couldn't take away all Bowie's resentment of the military; but the way she saw it, it would be good for all concerned if he let off a little steam on some piano keys.

"So go find some piano in an on-limits place and play for the people," Dana said suddenly. "And quit gaping at me like that!"

Bowie's eyebrows beetled. "Don't put me on about this, Da—"

"I'm not putting you on. Just remember: I gave Nova my word; I'm responsible for you. Don't mess up or we both take a fall. And sign back in at the barracks *before* midnight, read me?"

"Roger that," Bowie said, and was gone.

* * *

Feeling a good two kilos heavier after knocking back several more glasses, Dana (Bowie's gift orchid boutonniered to her uniform) returned to the barracks compound, left her Hovercycle in the mecha pool, and elevatored to the 15th's quarters. She looked in on Louie, but decided not to take him from his gadgeteering, and made for the ready-room, where she found Angelo nursing a drink in the dark, silently regarding the distant fortress, a black shape all but indiscernible from the ridgeline's numerous stone outcroppings and buttresses.

The sergeant sat with his arms folded, legs crossed, a sullen but contemplative look on his face. He was unaware of Dana's presence until she announced herself, asking to speak to him for a moment.

"About tomorrow's reconnaissance mission," they said simultaneously. But only Angelo chuckled.

Dana had serious issues on her mind now, the success of the mission, the safety of her team. With a bit of luck Bowie would land himself in the brig and she would be able to scratch him from her worry list. Sean and Louie presented no problems, and either of them could handle the squad's grunts; but that left Angelo Dante.

"I know this doesn't have to be said but once," Dana went on. "But... I know I can depend on you, Angie. Just wanted you to know."

"Same here, Lieutenant. Don't worry; we're gonna kick some alien butt."

It was typical of Angelo to put it this way: at the same time he was deferring to her and questioning her command abilities. *Alien* was directed at her; the sergeant's unmasked attack on her mixed ancestry. But she had lived with the "halfbreed" stigma for so long that it hardly fazed her anymore. Who on Earth hadn't lost someone to the Zentraedi wars? And with all of her mother's people aboard the SDF-3 or the Robotech Factory Satellite now, she was in effect the unofficial scapegoat for the unspeak-

able crimes of the past. If only Max and Miriya had foreseen this; she would have preferred death to the purga-
tory of the present.

"I'm aware of my responsibilities," she told Angelo.
"But I just wanted to say that this mission will fail even
before it gets under way unless you and I can begin to
trust each other."

She took the small orchid from her lapel, reached
across Angelo, and dropped it in his Scotch and soda.

"Hey—"

"Tropical ice," she smiled down at him. "A little good
luck charm for you, Angie—a peace offering. Do you
like it?"

"I guess . . ." the sergeant started to reply, sitting up in
his chair. But just then someone threw on the overhead
lights. Startled by the intrusion, he and Dana swung
around at the same moment to find Nova Satori and
Bowie centered in the wide doorway.

"I put you in charge of Bowie and this is what happens?" Nova said, as the entry doors slid shut.

Dana met them halfway, sizing up the situation quickly
and rehearsing her lines. She had certainly anticipated the
arrival of these two, but not Bowie's disheveled appearance. His uniform was soiled and one of his cheeks
looked bruised.

"Are you all right?" she asked him. "What's going on
here?"

Bowie wore a distressed look, more genuine than yesterday's.

"I guess I did it again," he answered contritely.

"I ought to throw you *both* in jail," Nova scolded
Dana. "He was in a barroom brawl." The lieutenant
looked like her namesake, ready to incinerate whatever
was in close proximity.

This time Nova herself had caught him red-handed,
following him from the café and waiting until just the
right moment to walk in on him. And now she had Dana

just where she wanted her: of course Nova would agree to release Bowie to her custody once again, but this time there would be a price to pay—a first look at the results of tomorrow's recon operation for starters. With rivalry increasing daily between Leonard's army intelligence and the Global Military Police, it was the only way Nova could count on getting the real dope.

Dana looked cross. "What was the fight about?"

"Ah, some loudmouth said no piano player is man enough to serve in the Hovertanks," Bowie admitted.

"That's a lot of rot!" Dana returned, back on Bowie's side all at once. "I wonder if *I'm* man enough?! I hope you taught him a lesson. I'm proud of you."

Nova expected as much, but played her part by growing angry.

"Go ahead, praise him, Lieutenant Sterling. You're digging his grave deeper."

"A soldier stands for something," Dana answered defensively. "What if somebody said no woman is good enough to be an MP—"

Nova wore a wry look. "Stuff the defense plea, Dana. Battles don't get won in barrooms, and merit doesn't get proven there either! What Bowie earned himself is a cell."

Unless we can cut a deal . . . Nova was saying to herself when Dana surprised her.

"All right then, take him away."

Both Bowie and Nova stared at her. The lieutenant's meticulously plucked eyebrows almost went up someplace into her hairline.

"Run him over to the guardhouse," Dana said evenly.

"B-but, Lieutenant, you can't be serious," Bowie burst out. Dana's verbal slap hurt more than that punch to the face. Even Angelo was stepping forward, coming to his aid, but Dana was unmoved.

"I have enough to handle without having to worry

about an eight ball," Dana said, trying not to think about the ochid in the drink glass, so nearby.

Nova was watching these exchanges with her mouth open. She gulped and found her voice, hoping she could salvage something from this. "Dana, you'd better not be kidding—"

Dana shook her head. "I've failed somewhere along the line . . . It's your turn to take care of him now." She caught the hurt look that surfaced in Bowie's eyes and turned away from him, determined to finish this scene no matter what.

"I've got to be on that mission tomorrow," Bowie was pleading with her. "You said I was right to defend our honor, now you're taking away my chance—"

She whirled on him suddenly. "I've heard it all before, Grant! You should have thought of that before you went off to that bar!"

Bowie's eyes went wide. "But Dana . . . *Lieutenant* . . . you—"

"Enough!" Dana cut him off. "Private Grant, ten-*hut*! You will accompany Lieutenant Satori to the stockade."

Nova's puzzlement increased. *Where had this one gone wrong?* "You don't want to reconsider. . . .?"

"My mind is made up."

Nova made a gesture of exasperation, then smiled in self-amusement and led Bowie away.

"What made you do that?" the sergeant asked Dana after they left. Having recently caught a glimpse of Bowie's sloppiness in the field, he wasn't opposed to Dana's decision but wondered, nevertheless, what had motivated this sudden attack.

"Because I'm CO here," Dana said evenly

CHAPTER
THREE

Thrilled at having received word of the 15th's mission to recon the alien ship—it never even occurred to me that she might not return!—I was suddenly faced with a new obstacle: Bowie Grant was in the custody of the GMP. Dana's reactions to the fortress were of paramount importance, but I was equally interested in establishing the depth of her involvement with the young Grant. I asked myself: Would proximity to the Masters reawaken her Zentraedi nature to the point where she would abandon her loyalties to both teammates and loved ones? It was therefore essential that Grant accompany the 15th, and up to me to see to it that Rolf Emerson learned of Grant's imprisonment.

Dr. Lazlo Zand, *Event Horizon: Perspectives on Dana Sterling and the Second Robotech War*

THE PENETRATION OPERATION GOT UNDER WAY early the next morning. Coordinated air strikes would provide the necessary diversion, and, with a bit of luck, the breach the 15th was going to require in order to infiltrate its dozen Hovertanks. Tech crews had worked all night long, going over the complex mecha systems and installing remote cameras.

General Emerson was monitoring the proceedings from the situation room. Staff officers and enlisted-ratings were buzzing in and out supplying him with updates and recon data. There were never less than six voices talking at the same time; but Emerson himself had little to say. He had his elbows on the table, fingers steepled, eyes fixed on the video transmissions relayed in by various spotter planes over the target zone. Only moments ago a combined team of Adventurer IIs and Falcon fighters had managed to awaken the apparently slumbering giant, and an intense firefight was in progress on the high ground surrounding the alien fortress. Armor-piercing rounds had thus far proved ineffective against the ship's layered hull, in spite of the fact that the XT's energy shield had yet to be deployed. But Emerson had just received word that the air corps was bringing in a QF-3000 E Ghost—an unmanned triple-cannon drone capable of delivering Reflex firepower of the sort that had proved effective in earlier airborne confrontations.

The wallscreen image of the besieged fortress derezzed momentarily, only to be replaced by a bird's-eye view of the 15th's diamond-formation advance. Emerson felt his pulse race as he watched the dozen mecha close on the heavily fortified perimeter. It was ironic that his attempts to deescalate the fledgling war had resulted in the 15th's assignment to this mission to hell; but in some ways he realized the perverted *rightness* of it: Emerson literally had to put what amounted to his family on the line in order to convince the supreme commander to listen to him. And Dana and Bowie were just that—family.

So often he would try to run his thoughts back in time, searching for the patterns that had led all of them to this juncture. Had there been signs along the way, omens he had missed, premonitions he had ignored? When the Sterlings and Grants had opted to leave aboard the SDF-3 as members of the Hunters' crew did it occur to them that they might not return from that corner of space ruled by the Robotech Masters, or that the Masters might come here instead? Emerson remembered the optimism that characterized those days, some fifteen years ago, when the newly-built ship had been launched, Rick and Lisa in command. Rolf and his wife had taken both Dana and infant Bowie: After all, they had so often watched over the kids while the Grants spent time on the Factory

Satellite, and the Sterlings combed the jungles of the Zentraedi Control Zone—what used to be called Amazonia—for Malcontents; it seemed a perfect solution then that the kids should remain here while their parents embarked on the Expeditionary Mission that was meant to return peace to the galaxy. . .

That Emerson had chosen to enroll both of them in the military had resulted in a divorce from his wife. Laura never understood his reasons; childless herself, Dana and Bowie had become her children, and what mother—what *parent!*—would choose to wish war on her offspring? But Rolf was merely honoring the promises he had made to Vince and Jean, Max and Miriya. Perhaps each of them did have a sense of what the future held, and perhaps they reasoned that the kids would have a better chance on Earth than they would, lost in space? Certainly they recognized why Rolf had decided to remain behind, just as surely as Supreme Commander Leonard recognized it. . . .

Emerson pressed his hands to his face, fingers massaging tired eyes. When he looked up again, Lieutenant Milton, an energetic young aide, was standing over his right shoulder. Milton saluted and bent close by his shoulder to report that Bowie was in the guardhouse. It seemed that the GMP had caught him involved in a barroom brawl.

Rolf nodded absently, watching the displays, and thinking of a little boy who had cried so inconsolably when his parents left him behind. He wondered whether Bowie had purposely provoked a fight in order to absent himself from the mission. He had to be made to understand that rules were meant to be followed. The 15th had been chosen and as a member of that team he owed it to the others. Of course, it was equally plausible that Dana was behind this; she didn't seem to comprehend that her overprotectiveness wasn't doing Bowie any good, either.

"Tell Lieutenant Satori that General Emerson would consider it a personal favor if she could find a way to release Private Grant," Rolf told his aide in low tones.

"Ask her for me to see to it that Bowie rejoins his unit as soon as possible."

The lieutenant saluted and left in a rush as Emerson returned his attention to the wallscreen's bird's-eye view of the 15th's advance, realizing all at once that Bowie's readdition to the team would raise their number to *thirteen*.

The terrain between Monument City and the fortress was as rugged as it came. What was formerly a series of wooded slopes rising from a narrow river valley had been transformed by Dolza's annihilation bolts into a tortuous landscape of eroded crags and precipitous outcroppings, denuded, waterless, and completely unnatural. Stretches of ancient highways could be seen here and there beneath deposits of pulverized granite, or volcanic earthworks.

Before dawn the 15th was in position just below the fortress's crash site, ringed as it was on three sides by pseudobuttes and tors. Dana had brought the column to a halt, awaiting the arrival of the Ghost drone. Quiet reigned on all fronts.

Cocooned in the mecha's cockpit, her body sheathed from head to foot in armor, she sensed a strange assemblage of feelings vying for her attention. By rights her mind should have been emptied, rendered fully accessible to the mecha's reconfiguration demands; but with things at a temporary impasse, she gave inner voice to some of these thoughts.

She knew, for example, that the thrill she felt was attributable to her Zentraedi ancestry; the fear, her Human one. But this was hardly a clear-cut case of ambivalence or dichotomy; rather she experienced an odd commin gling of the two, where each contained a measure of its opposite. Her heart told her that inside the fortress she would encounter her own reflection: the racial past she had been told about but never experienced. How had her mother felt when going into combat against her own brothers and sisters? Dana asked herself. Or when hunting down the giant Malcontents who roamed the wastelands? No different, she supposed, than when a Human went to war against his or her own kind. But would it ever end? Even her fun-loving uncles—Rico, Konda, and Bron—were resigned to warfare in the end, telling her before they died that peace, when it came, would merely be an interlude in the War Without End. . . .

Beside her now, a Hovertank unexpectedly joined the 15th's front ranks, raising a cloud of yellow dust as it slid to a halt in the pebbly earth. Dana thought the Battloid's head through a left turn and almost jumped free of her seat straps when she recognized the mecha as Bowie's *Diddy-Wa-Diddy.*

"What in world are you doing here, Private?" she barked over the tac net.

"You tell me. Somebody sprang me."

"Good ole Uncle Rolf." She let the bitterness be heard in her tone. Emerson had undermined her command.

"That's the way I figured it," Bowie laughed. Then the laughter was gone. "And Private Grant is completely at your service. I've learned my lesson, Dana."

Rolf! Dana thought.

Infuriated, she began to hatch sinister plots against him, but the scenarios all played themselves out rather quickly. Rolf was thinking of Bowie's self-image, as always, and she couldn't help but understand. It was just that self-image wouldn't count for much if you didn't live to cash in on it. *Or would it? . . .* Senseless to debate it now, she told herself as the cockpit displays lit up.

"Then fall in, trooper!" she told Bowie.

"No more a' this eight-ball crap," Dana heard Angelo second over the net.

"I copy, Sarge," Bowie said.

Dana called in air strikes as the 15th got moving again, straight for the colossal alloy rampart that was the flagship's hull.

Scoop-nosed Tac Air fighters, Adventurers and Falcons, came down in prearranged sorties, dumping tons of smart and not-so-smart ordnance, strafing, braving the fire of the glassy inverted-teardrop fortress cannon. Warheads exploded violently against the ship's hull, summoning in return thundering volleys of pulse-cannon fire and an outpouring of Bioroids, some on foot, but many more atop ordnance-equipped hovercraft. Ground teams peppered the existing alien troops with chaingunfire, and the tac net erupted in a cacophony of commands, requests, praise, and blood-curdling screams.

While the two sides exchanged death, the Ghost drone dropped in on its release run. A nontransformable hybrid of the Falcon and the Veritech, the Ghost was developed in the early stages of Robotechnology as an adjunct to the transorbital weapons system utilized by the Armor series orbital platforms. It had undergone several modifications since, and the one in present use was closer to a smart bomb than a drone aircraft. Professor Miles Cochran's team had plotted an impact point toward the bow of the fortress, in the vertical portion of hull somewhat below the pyramidal structure known to some as Louie's "Robotech Teat."

ATAC Battloids took up firing positions and concentrated their total power on the predesignated section of the hull in an attempt to soften it up. Main batteries and rifle/cannon, and the multiple barrels of the secondaries, everything in the 15th cut loose, aimed at the one small section of offworld alloy. The air shimmered and cooked away; heat waves rose all around, and power levels in the ATACs dropped rapidly. Dana sweated and hoped that no assault ship or Bioroid came at them now, when the 15th's mecha must hold their positions until the breach had been made.

Sterling kept the 15th well back from the strike zone as the Ghost zeroed in. The craft fell short of its projected goal, but the ensuing explosion proved powerful enough to open a fiery hole large enough to accommodate a Hovertank, and no one could ask for more than that.

The ATACs lowered their weapons in a kind of shocked surprise.

"When we get back, I'll buy the beers!" Bowie said, breaking the silence.

Dana returned an invisible smile and thanked him, promising to hold him to his word. "All right, Fifteenth," she commanded over the tac net, "you know the drill!"

Protoculture worked its magic as Battloids mechamorphosed to Hovertank mode, reconfiguring like some exotic, knightly origami. Thrusters whined as the tanks floated into formation, forming up on Dana for the recon, and riding separate blasting carpets toward the jagged opening and the dark unknown.

Behind the visor of her *Valkyrie*'s helmet, Dana Sterling's eyes narrowed. "Now we take the war to *them*!" she said.

The Bioroids didn't exactly escort the 15th in, nor welcome them with open arms once they arrived. Dana raised the canopy of her mecha and gestured the team forward, ordering them over the net to maintain formation. She led them on a beeline to the breach, disc gun and cannon fire paving an explosive road for the Hovertanks, which continued to loose pulsed bursts in return. Miraculously, though, no one was hit and shortly the 15th found itself inside one of the fortress's cavernous chambers.

It was Professor Cochran's suggestion—based on a rather sketchy analysis of the fortress's infrastructure (which had led him to believe that much of the starboard holds were given over to defense and astrogation)—that the team swing itself toward the port side of the ship if possible. This quickly proved to be not only viable but necessary because the starboard section was found partitioned off by a massive bulkhead it would have taken another Ghost to breach. Consequently, the ATACs barely cut their speed as they advanced.

Three Bioroids suddenly appeared, dropping from overhead circular portals that simply weren't there a moment before—"They may as well have dropped in from another dimension," Louie Nichols would say later.

As annihilation discs flew past Dana's head, she trained the *Valkyrie*'s muzzle on the first of these and took it out with a faceplate shot; the alien seemed to absorb the cranial round silently, slumping down and shorting out as Dana sped past it. The other two were laying down a steady stream of crippling fire most of the team managed to avoid. But Dana then heard a terror-filled scream pierce the net and saw one of the 15th's tanks screeching along the vast corridor on its hind end. Dante was trying to raise Private Simon when the mecha barreled into one of the Bioroids and exploded. Dana and Louie poured plasma against the remaining one, literally blowing it limb from limb.

"Status report!" the lieutenant demanded when they brought the tanks to a halt.

The corridor, a good fifteen-meters wide, was filled with thick smoke and littered with mecha debris. The severed arm of a Bioroid lay twitching on the floor, leaking a sickly green fluid and a worm's nest of wires. Dana wondered what sort of reception HQ was receiving and tried without success to raise them on the radio. Display sensors gave no indication that the video units were incapacitated, so she swiveled the camera through a 360 for Emerson's benefit. Louie, meanwhile, launched a self-deployed monitoring unit.

It was Simon's mecha that had collided with the Bioroid. Fortunately, the private had bailed out at the last minute, his armor protecting him from the explosion and what would have been a full-body road rash. However, without the mecha, Dana informed him, he was going to be useless to the team.

"But why?" he was saying to her now. "It's not my fault my craft was disabled."

Sean, Road, and Woodruff had positioned themselves as a rear guard; Angelo, Bowie, and Louie were forward. Private Jordon and the rest of the team had dismounted and were grouped around Dana and Simon, the helmetless private looking small and defenseless in the vastness of the corridor. Jordon, who rarely knew when to keep his mouth shut, suddenly found it necessary to back up Dana's words to Simon.

"You just have to understand, Simon, we can't afford to jeopardize the mission by dragging you along with us."

Meanwhile, Dana had been trying to figure out just what she could do with Simon. They were a good half mile in, certainly not too far from the breach to have him leg it back, but what could he do when he got there? The skirmish was still in progress and he wouldn't stand a chance outside. He could ride second in one of the tanks, but Dana thought it was best to post Simon and one of the others here as backup. Jordon was as good a choice as any.

Jordon didn't take the news any better than Simon had, but Dana put a quick end to his protests. He and Simon were to wait for the team to return; if no one returned by 0600 hours they were to try and raise HQ and make their own way out of the fortress. In the meantime, Dana would see to it that Louie maintained radio contact with them every thirty minutes. With that, she regrouped the rest of the 15th and signaled them forward.

A substantial portion of their premission briefing had involved a thorough study of the archive notes left by the men who had reconned the first super dimensional fortress shortly after its fateful arrival on Earth. That group had been led by Henry Gloval and Dr. Emil Lang, and had also included the legendary Roy Fokker and the now notorious T. R. Edwards. But the 15th found little simi-

larity between what they had read and what they were
faced with now. For starters, the SDF-1 group had gone
in on foot; but more important, this ship was *known to be
armed and dangerous*. All Dana could do was keep
proper procedure in mind and try to emulate Gloval's me-
thodical approach.

As a group they continued at moderate speed along
the dimly lit corridor, the height and width of which never
varied. It was hexagon-shaped, although somewhat elongated vertically, a constant fifteen-yards wide across the
floor—uniform blue outsized tiles—by some twenty-five
yards high. The walls (paneled on the downward slope
and strangely variegated and cell-like above) appeared to
be constructed of a laser-resistant ceramic. There was no
ceiling as such, save for a continuum of enormous tie
beams, proportionally spaced, beyond which lay an im-
penetrable thicket of pipes, conduits, and tubing—an unending knot of capillaries and arterial junctures. But by
far the most interesting objects in the corridor were the
adornments that lined the upper walls of the hexagon—
oval shaped, ruby-red opaque lenses spaced five meters
apart along the entire length of the hall. Every twelfth
medallion was a more ornate version, backed by a segmented cross with pointed arms. Twice, the 15th entered
a stretch of corridor where these lenses found their match
in similar convexities that lined the lower walls, but along
one side only.

The team was moving parallel to the long axis of the
fortress, one mile in when they reached the first fork, a
symmetrical Y-shaped intersection at the end of a long
sweeping curve, with identical corridors branching off left
and right. The archway was lined with a kind of segmented trimwork that looked soft and inviting, but was in
fact ceramic like the walls. Here, the servo-gallery above
the openwork ceiling was bathed in infrared light.

Dana once again ordered them to a halt and split the

team: the sergeant would take the B team—Marino, Xavez, Kuri, and Road—into the left fork; Dana, Corporal Nichols and the rest of the 15th would explore the right.

"We'll rendezvous back here in exactly two hours," she said to Angelo from the open cockpit. "Okay, move out."

Dante's group swung their vehicles out of formation and followed the sergeant's slow lead into the corridor. Dana gave a wave and the A team fell in behind her tank. Behind the 15th, unseen, three curious, Human-size figures stealthily crossed the corridor. One of them depressed a ruby-red button that seemed part of a medallion's design. From pockets concealed in the archway slid five concentrically-etched panels of impervious metal, sealing off the corridor.

Dana's group passed quickly through domed chambers, empty and discomforting, with riblike support trusses and walls like stretched skin. Beyond that was the selfsame hexagonal corridor and yet another Y intersection.

"Which way now?" Bowie asked.

Dana was against breaking the team up into yet smaller groups, but they had to make the most of their time. "Bowie, you and Louie come with me down the right corridor," she said after a moment. "Sean, you and the others take the left one—got it?"

While Dana was issuing the orders, Bowie happened to glance over his shoulder—in time to see what appeared to be the retreating shadow of a being of some sort. But the light here was so unsettling that he resisted alarming the others; his eyes had been playing tricks on him since they entered the fortress and he didn't want the team to think him paranoid. Nevertheless, Dana caught his sharp intake of breath and asked him what he had seen.

"Just my imagination, Lieutenant," he told her as

Sean's group split off and moved their Hovertanks into the left corridor.

Dana also had the feeling that they were being watched—how could it *not* be so, given the techno-systems of the ship? But that was all right: *she wanted to be seen.*

The right corridor proved to be a new world: hexagonal still, but fully enclosed, with an overhead "bolstered" ridge and numerous riblike trusses. Gone were the medallions and ruby ovals; the walls, upper and lower, were an unbroken series of rectangular light panels. A new world, but a worrisome one.

Without success, Dana tried to raise Sergeant Dante on the net.

"I haven't been able to raise him, either," Louie said, a note of distress in his voice. "Do you think we should go look for him?"

Dana was considering this when the silence that had thus far accompanied them was suddenly broken by a distant sound of servo-motors slamming and clanking into operation. The three teammates turned around and watched as a solid panel began its steady descent from overhead.

The corridor was sealing itself off!

Ahead of them, a second door was descending; and beyond that a third, and fourth. As far as they could see, massive curtains of armor-plate were dropping from pockets built into the ceiling trusses, echos of descent and closure filling the air.

"Hit it!" Dana exploded. "Full power!"

The Hovertanks shot forward at top speed, barely clearing the first gate. They tore beneath a dozen more in the same fashion, seemingly gaining on the progression— three urban joyriders beating the traffic lights downtown.

Then all at once the progression shifted: up ahead of them was a fully closed gate. Dana, far out in front of

Bowie and Louie, reached for her retro levers and pulled them home, favoring the port throttle so that the hind end of the tank gradually began to come around to starboard. There was no way in the world she wanted to hit that gate head-on. . . .

CHAPTER
FOUR

*Initial analysis of the fruit [found aboard the alien fortress]
revealed little more than its basic structure—its similarities to
certain tropical fruits seldom seen in northern markets these
days. But subsequent tests proved intriguing: one taste of the
fruit and a laboratory chimp soared into what Cochran described as "a one-way ticket to reverie." And yet it was not a
true hallucinogen; in fact, molecular scans showed it to be
closer to animal than vegetal in makeup!... Several years
would go by before our questions would be answered.*

Mingtao, *Protoculture: Journey Beyond Mecha*

THE HUGE WALLSCREEN IN THE SITUATION ROOM WAS
little more than static bars and snow. A flicker of image
enlivened it momentarily, incomprehensibly, then there
was nothing.

"We've lost contact with the Fifteenth," a tech reported to General Emerson.

"Increase enhancement," Rolf said sternly, bent on
denying the update. "See if you can raise them."

Haltingly a second tech turned to the task, well aware
of what the results would be. "Negatory," he said to
Emerson after a moment. "I'm afraid the interference is
overwhelming."

Colonel Anderson pivoted in his seat to face Rolf.
"Should we consider sending in a rescue team?"

Emerson shook his head but said nothing. *The loss of
one team would be enough... the loss of two loved ones,
more than he could bear.* He pressed his hands to his face,
fearing the worst....

* * *

The left corridor had led Sergeant Dante's contingent to an enormous hold filled with a bewildering array of Robotech machinery.

"Where is Louie when you need him," Angelo was saying to his men.

They had all dismounted from their Hovertanks and were grouped together marveling at the chamber's wonders. The hold was simply too spacious to fathom, its distant horizons lost in darkness. Here was a massive cone-shaped generator, three hundred yards in circumference if it was an inch; there, a second generator harnessing and shunting energy the likes of which Dante had never seen—a raw subatomic fire that seemed to have a life of its own. Liquids alive as fresh blood pulsed through transparent pipes, coursing from generator to generator, machine to machine, while unattended display screens strobed amber-lit schematics to robot readers, communicating to one another through a cacophonous language of shrill sounds and harsh rasps.

There was no telling how high the hold went: indeterminate levels of conduits, tubes, and mains crisscrossed overhead, illuminated by flashes of infrared light projected by spherical anti-grav Cyclopean remotes—ruby-eyed monitors, ribbed and whiskered with segmented antennae.

"Look at the size of this place!" Private Road exclaimed. (Angelo couldn't wait to promote the guy just to put an end to the running joke.)

"Hold it down," said the sergeant. "Stay alert and keep your eyes peeled for anything that might be threatening."

"Threatening?" Marino asked in disbelief, his assault rifle welded to his hands. "This whole place looks pretty threatening to me, Sarge."

"Gimme hell anyday," Xavez seconded.

Dante whirled on both of them, raising his voice. "I

said can it, and I'm not gonna tell you again! The next guy that speaks is gonna be in a sorrier scene than this! Now, spread out! But keep in sight of each other! We've gotta job to do."

High above them, one of the eyeball remotes blinked, fixing an aerial image of men and mecha in its fish-eye lens. That much accomplished, the device rotated slightly and emitted a patterned series of light.

On a gallery still higher up in the hold, the code was received by a shadowy creature, which acknowledged the signal and moved off into the darkness.

Private Road, meanwhile, had begun to edge away from the tight-knit group. There was no sense waiting around for the sarge to wrap up his lecture—they could recite it from memory by now, even the threats and imprecations. The private smiled in the privacy of his face shield and took a small step backwards. But suddenly something was taking him a step further: a vice had been clamped around his throat, shutting down his oxygen supply and crushing the nascent scream that was lodged in his throat. He could feel his eyeballs begin to swell and protrude as whatever had him increased the torque of its grip. He heard and felt the snap that broke his neck, the rush of death in his ears. . . .

". . . and I want you to sound off the minute you see anything suspicious," Angelo finished up. He had armed his weapon and was lowering his face shield when Kuri made a puzzled sound over the tac net.

"Hey Sarge, Road's gone."

Dante leveled his weapon and swung toward where he had last seen the private. Xavez and Marino exchanged wary looks, then followed the sergeant's lead.

"Road!" Dante called softly. He dropped his mask and called him again through the net. When there was no response, he gestured briefly to the team. "All right, don't just stand there: find him!" To Kuri he said: "See if you can raise the lieutenant."

Dante double-checked his weapon, thinking: *If this is Road's idea of a joke, they'll be calling him dead-end from now on!*

Suddenly, without warning, the room was sectioned by laser fire.

"Stand clear!" Dana warned Bowie and Louie.

The two of them returned to their Hovertanks as Dana primed the laser and aimed it at the armored gate.

Dana's mecha had managed to stop just short of the thing, hind end almost fully around, two meters from collision. She had repositioned it in the center of the corridor now, thirty meters from the gate. The barrier was some sort of high-density metal, unlike the durceramic of the corridor walls, and Louie had every confidence that the laser would do the trick.

"Any luck raising Sergeant Dante or Jordon?" Dana asked Louie once more before targeting.

Louie shook his head and flashed her a thumbs-down.

"Even my optic sensor is out," he told her over the net.

That didn't surprise her, given the apparent thickness of the corridor walls and the fact that they were at least one-and-a-half miles into the fortress by now. Nor did the barriers come as any great shock; all along she had sensed that their progress was being monitored.

"Do you think they caught the others?" Bowie said worriedly.

"Your guess is as good as mine," she responded casually, and turned her attention to the laser. "All right then: here goes."

She depressed the laser's trigger; there was enough residual smoke in the corridor to give her a glimpse of the light-ray itself, but by and large her eyes were glued to the barrier. Louie had cautioned her that it would prove to be a tedious operation—a slow burn they would probably need to help along with an armor-piercing round—

but Louie was not infallible: instead of that expected slow burn, the laser blew a massive hole in the gate on impact.

"Well that wasn't so bad," Dana said when the shrapnel-storm passed.

She reached for her rifle, dismounted the tank, and approached the gate cautiously. Beyond it was a short stretch of corridor that opened into what she guessed was the fortress's water-recycling and ventilation hold. What with the numerous shafts and ducts here, she reasoned she couldn't be far off the mark.

"What do you see, Lieutenant?" Louie asked from behind her.

Dana lifted her face shield. "Not much of anything, but at least we're out of that trap." As Bowie and Louie caught up with her, she cautioned them to stay together.

There were enough dripping sounds, sibilant rushes, and roars to make them feel as though they had entered a giant's basement. But there was something else as well: almost a wind-chime's voice, soft and atonal, all but lost to their ears but registering nonetheless as if through some sixth sense. It seemed to fill the air, and yet have no single source, ambient as full-moon light. At times it reminded Dana of bells or gongs, but no sooner would she fix on that, than the sound would reconfigure and appear harplike or string percussive.

"It's like music," Bowie said to a transfixed Dana.

The sound was working on her, infiltrating her, *playing* her, as though *she* were the instrument: her music was memory's song, but dreamlike, preverbal and impossible to hold. . . .

"Are you all right, Lieutenant?" Louie was asking her, breaking the spell.

She encouraged the tone to leave her, and suggested they try to locate the source of the sound. Louie, his face shield raised, ever-present goggles in place, had his ear pressed to one of the hold's air ducts. He motioned Dana and Bowie over, and the three of them crouched around the duct, listening intently for a moment.

"Maybe it's just faulty plumbing," Bowie suggested.

Louie ignored the jest. "This is the first sign of life we've encountered. We have to figure out where it's coming from and how to get to it."

Dana stood up, wondering just how they could accomplish that. Excited by the discovery, Louie was firing questions at her faster than she could field them. She silenced him and returned her attention to the sound; when she looked up again, Louie was falling through the wall.

Sean and company—Woodruff and Cranston—were in what appeared to be some sort of "hot house," scarcely 200 yards from the water-recycling chamber (though they had no way of knowing this), but in any case separated from the lieutenant's contingent by three high-density ceramic bulkheads. "Hot house" was Sean's conjecture, just as recycling chamber had been Dana's, but it had taken the private several minutes to come up with even this description.

There was no soil, no hydroponic cultivation bins or artificial sunlight, no water vapor or elevated oxygen or carbon dioxide levels; only row after row of alien plants that seemed to be growing upside down. Central to each was an almost incandescent globe, some ten meters in circumference, tendriled and supported by, or perhaps suspended from, groupings of rigid, bristly lianalike vines. (Cranston was reminded of the macrame plant hangers popular in the last century, although he didn't mention this to the others.) The globes themselves were positioned anywhere from five to fifteen meters from the floor of the chamber, and below them, both still affixed to the stalks themselves or spread about the floor, were individual fruits, the size of apples but the red of strawberries.

The three men had left their idling Hovertanks to have

a closer look. Sean had the face shield of his helmet raised, and was casually flipping one of the fruits in his hand, using elbow snaps to propel the thing in the air. Talk had switched from the plants themselves to the fact that the team had yet to encounter any resistance. No one had taken the dare to taste the fruit, but Sean had thought to stow a few ripe specimens in his tank for later analysis.

"It's crazy," the one-hand juggler was saying now. "They were awful anxious to keep us out of here in the first place, so why are they so quiet now?"

"Maybe we frightened them?" Cranston suggested. "Up close, I mean," he hastened to add after catching the look Sean threw him.

"W-w-what d'ya guys got against peace and quiet anyway?" Woodruff stammered.

Sean made a wry face. "Nothing, Jack. Except when it's *too* quiet, like it is right now. We just can't let ourselves be lulled by it, is all. Or else they'll be all over us." Sean held the fruit out in front of him and began to squeeze it. "Like this!" he said, as the fruit ruptured, releasing a thick white juice that touched all of them.

It was actually a hinged, polygonal section of wall that Louie Nichols had fallen through. And behind it were even stranger surprises.

At sight of the first of these—a rectangular vat filled with assorted body parts floating in a viscous lavender solution—Louie almost blew his breakfast, his eyes going wide beneath the tinted goggles. Bowie and Dana stepped in and followed his lead, registering their revulsion in stifled exclamations and sounds.

A five-fingered grappling claw was attached to the side of the vat, its purpose immediately obvious to Louie as he took in the rest of the room. Behind them was a conveyor belt, also equipped with a grappling arm, and a tableful of artificial heads.

"It's an assembly line!" Bowie said in disbelief. "And we thought these aliens were humanoid!"

"Mustn't jump to conclusions," Louie cautioned him, leaning toward the tank now and reaching forward to touch the arms and legs floating there. He was fully composed again, curious and fascinated. "These are android parts," he said after a moment of scrutiny, amazement in his voice.

Dana decided to risk another look and watched as the corporal pulled and probed at the ligamentlike innards of a forearm and the artificial flesh of a face.

"Incredible," Louie pronounced. "The texture is actually *lifelike*. It isn't cold or metallic . . . They seem to have developed a perfect bio-mechanical combinant. . . ."

Bowie, feeling a little like a corpuscle in a lymph node, had wandered away from the vat to investigate the membrane walls of the room—any excuse to absent himself from Louie's continuing anatomy lesson. But even so, words from his science courses kept creeping into his thoughts: *cell-wall*, *vacuole*, *nucleus* . . . A minute later—during an elevator ascent through thin air—he would recall that *osmosis* was the last thing he had said to himself before being sucked through the wall. . . .

He also told himself that it was useless to struggle against this new situation: stepping off the radiant disk under his feet or propelling himself clear of the globe of soft light encompassing him seemed like risky ventures at the moment, and for all he knew this ride would land him outside the fortress, topside, smack dab in the middle of all that fighting and strafing, which was fine with him—

But all at once those dreams of an easy out came to an abrupt end, along with the disk itself. Bowie picked himself up off the floor—thankful there was one—and brought his assault rifle up, shouting demands into white-light fog: "All right—what's going on here?!"

He was answered by the music they had heard in the water-recycling hold, who knew how many levels below him now. Only it was much more present here and, he realized, haunting and beautiful. He lowered the helmet's face shield and took one cautious step forward into the radiant haze, then a second and third. Several more and he began to discern the bounderies of the light; there was a corridor beyond, similar to those hexagonal ones they had already negotiated but on a smaller scale. The walls were textured, bare except for the occasional ruby-colored oval medallion, and the floor shone like polished marble. There was also a dead end to this particular windsong-filled corridor, or, as it turned out, a doorway.

Twin panels that formed the hexagonal portal slid apart as Bowie made his approach, revealing a short hall adorned with two opposing rows of Romanesque columns, medallioned like the walls. Overhead ran a continuous, arched skylight, hung with identical fixtures along its length—cluster representations of some red, apple-sized fruit. Shafts of sunlight danced along the hall's seamless floor.

Following the sound, Bowie turned left into a perpendicular hall, with curved sides and proportionately spaced rib trusses. The music was still stronger here, emanating, it seemed, from a dark room off to Bowie's right. Bowie hesitated at the entry, rechecked his weapon, and stepped through.

In the dark he saw a woman seated at a monitor—a curiously shaped device like everything on this ship, Bowie told himself—an up-ended clamshell, strung like a harp with filaments of colored light. The woman, on the other hand, was heavenly shaped: somewhat shorter than Bowie, with straight deep green hair that would have reached her knees if loosed from the ringlet that held it full halfway down her back. She was dressed in some sort of sky-blue, clinging chiffon bodysuit, with a coral-colored gauzelike cape and bodice wrapping that left one shoulder bare. She had her small hands positioned at the light-controls of the device when she turned and took notice of Bowie's entry. And it was only then—as her hands froze and the music began to waver—that Bowie realized she was *playing* the device: *She was the source of the music!*

He recognized at once that he had frightened her and moved quickly to soften his aspect, shouldering his weapon and keeping his voice calm as he spoke to her.

"Don't be scared. Is that better?" he asked, gesturing to his now slung rifle. "Believe me, you have nothing to fear from me." Bowie risked a small step toward her. "I just wanted to compliment you on your playing. I'm a musician myself."

She sat unmoving in the harp's equally unusual seat, her eyes wide and fixed on him. Bowie kept up the patter, noticing details as he approached: the thick band she wore on her right wrist, the fact that the hair bracketing her innocent face was cut short. . . .

"So you see we have something in common. They say that music is the universal language—"

Suddenly she was on her feet, ready to run, and Bowie stopped short. "Easy now," he repeated. "I'm not a monster. I'm just a person—like you." As he heard himself, he imagined how he must appear to her in his helmet and full-body armor. He rid himself of the "thinking cap" and saw her relax some. Encouraged, he introduced himself and asked for her name, tried a joke about being deaf, and finally dropped himself into the harp's cushioned, highbacked chair.

"I'm forgetting that music is the universal language," he said, turning to the instrument itself and wondering where to begin. "Maybe this'll work," he smiled up at the green-haired girl, who stood puzzled beside him, taking in all his words but uttering nothing in return.

Bowie regarded the ascending strings of light, marveling at shifting patterns of color. He positioned his hands in the harp, palms downward, interrupting the flow. As the tones changed, he tried to discern some correlation between the colors and sounds, thinking back to obscure musical texts he had read, the occult schools' approach to Pythagorean correspondences . . . Still he could make no musical sense of this harp. And it was soon apparent that the harpist herself could make no sense of Bowie's attempts.

"How long has it been since you had this thing tuned?" he said playfully, as the woman leaned in to demonstrate.

Bowie watched her intently, more fascinated by her sudden closeness than the richness of her music. But as her graceful hands continued to stroke the light-strings, Bowie felt a soothing magic begin to work on him, eliciting feelings he could not define, other than to say that the harpist and her instrument were the source of them; that it felt as though *he could somehow be made to do the harp's bidding.*

"That's the most beautiful thing I've ever heard," Bowie said softly. "And you're the most beautiful thing I've ever seen."

She had scarcely acknowledged his earlier attempts at verbal communication, but this seemed to give her pause; she turned from the harp to stare at him, as though his words were music she could understand.

Then all at once the room was flooded with light.

Startled back to reality, Bowie leapt up from the seat, his helmet crashing to the floor, as a raspy synthesized voice said, "Don't make a move, Earthling."

Bowie reached for his rifle, nevertheless, snarling "trap" to both the harpist and the armored shock troopers who had burst into the room.

"Don't be a fool," cautioned the second trooper.

Bowie saw the wisdom of this and moved his hands clear of his weapon. It was difficult to know whether there were humanoids inside the gleaming armor worn by the aliens, but Bowie sensed that these troopers had been assembled from the android parts he had seen only a short time ago. This pair was human-size, armed with featureless laser rifles, and encased in helmets and cumbersome body armor, including long carapacelike capes that stood stiffly out behind them.

"Another move and it will be your last. You're coming with us—*now*. You, too, Musica."

Bowie turned at the sound of her name, and repeated it for Musica's benefit. He thought he detected the beginnings of a smile before one of the android's said: "All right, Earthman, come along quietly now"—as though lifting dialogue from an archaic motion picture.

Bowie sized up the two of them: they were side by side, perhaps three yards from him, gesturing with their rifles, but more intent on capturing him than blowing him away. Spying his helmet on the floor now, Bowie saw an opportunity and went for it. He took a step forward, as though surrendering to them, then quickly brought his right foot against the helmet, launching it square into the face of one of the androids, while pile-driving himself into the other one. The trooper took the full force of his blow and staggered backward but remained on its feet. Bowie was clutching the thing like a tackle when he saw that number one had come around and had the rifle leveled on him. He sucked in his breath and slipped out of the clutches of the second, just as number one fired, catching his companion through the face with several rounds. Both Bowie and the android were motionless for a brief moment while the weight of this reversal descended; then Bowie had his own rifle out front and put several rounds in the suddenly speechless alien. The trooper dropped to the floor with a thud.

Bowie turned to Musica and threw his shoulders back triumphantly. But this was no green-haired Rapunzel he had just rescued, and it didn't occur to him that he had just aced two of her people. Musica, her hands like nervous birds, was staring at him distressfully, backing slowly away, as if expecting the next round to come zinging her way.

Bowie finally realized what was going on and tried to persuade her that he had done her some sort of favor. "Don't tell me you're still afraid of me?" he said, putting his hands on her shoulders while she buried her face in her hands. "I saved you from those two, didn't I? Doesn't that prove I'm your friend?"

Musica was whimpering, shaking her head back and forth while he spoke; but still he went on: "Now all we have to do is get out of here.... Can you show me the way?"

She finally succeeded in tearing herself away from him and began to run. Bowie was starting after her when all at once a blast rang out from behind both of them catching Musica unawares in the calf. Bowie caught up and supported her, thinking that she had been trying to warn him. He looked back toward the trooper who had loosed the shot: the android was on its knees now, but there would be no need for Bowie to waste a charge against it. In a second the thing was going to topple facedown of its own accord.

But again the mistress of the harp broke free and ran, this time though a blue and red triskelionlike doorway—some ultra modernist hexagonal painting that slid apart into three sections as she approached, and closed just as quickly behind her.

Bowie tore after her and found himself back in the columned hallway, but Musica was nowhere in sight. Then he chanced to look to the right and there she was: casually entering the hall from a perpendicular corridor.

"Well, that's better!" Bowie said smiling.

But off she went again and the chase was on.

"Take it easy," Bowie shouted after her, breathlessly. "You shouldn't be running on that wounded leg." What he really meant to say was that it wasn't fair of her to be outrunning him, but he was hoping that a demonstration of concern for her well-being might prove more effective than an admission of defeat. But then he noticed that her leg showed no signs of the wound he had definitely seen there only a minute before. And come to think of it, he found himself wondering: wasn't her hair more green than the blue he was seeing now?

The intersections and branchings grew more and more numerous, a veritable labyrinth of hexagonal corridors, polished replicas of the ones belowdecks, with medallioned walls and stark blood-red ceiling panels seemingly filled with axons and dendrites.

Bowie lost her in a maze of twists and turns. He stood still, breathing hard and fast, listening for any sound of her. But what he heard instead was the approach of something large and motorized. He brought his rifle off his shoulder and moved to the center of the corridor, waiting to confront whatever was about to show itself from around the bend.

CHAPTER
FIVE

Did you ever see a dream walking?
Well, Bowie did.

Remark attributed to Angelo Dante

IN AN ORGANICALLY-FASHIONED CHAMBER LONG AGO given over to the demands of the Protoculture, the Masters observed the Humans who had been allowed access to their ship. The rubylike corridor adornments Louie had called medallions were their eyes and ears, and when the humans had strayed from these, the Masters had relied on intelligence gathered by their android troopers, the Terminators—the same armored beings who had almost gotten the drop on Bowie and were presently exchanging fire with Sergeant Dante's contingent, still trapped in the generator hold, one of their number already dead.

The trio of aged Masters was in its steadfast position at the shrub-sized mushroom-shaped device that was their interface with the physical world. In many ways slaves to this Protoculture cap, generations past the need for food or sustenance, the Masters lived only for the cerebral rewards of that interior realm, lived only for the Protoculture itself, and their fleeting contact with worlds beyond imagining.

But though evolved to this high state, they were not permanent residents in that alternate reality, and so had to compromise their objectives to suit the needs of the crumbling empire they had forged when control really was in their hands. This mission to Earth had proved to be as troublesome as it was desperate, a last chance for the Masters of Tirol to regain what they needed most— the Protoculture matrix Zor had hidden aboard the now ruined super dimensional fortress. The Masters were not interested in destroying the insignificant planet that had been the unwitting recipient of their renegade scientist's dubious gift; but neither were they about to allow this primitive race to stand between them and destiny; between them and *immortality*.

At this stage of the Masters' game there was still some curiosity at work: viewing the Earthlings was akin to having a look at their own past—before the Protoculture had so reconfigured fate—which is why they had permitted this small band of Terrans into the fortress to begin with. Earthlings had thus far proved themselves an aggressive lot: firing on the Masters when they had first appeared and goading them into further exchanges, as if intent upon ushering in the doomsday the Zentraedi had been unable to provide.

But perhaps this was but a measure of their stunted development? And this small reconnaissance party was nothing more than an attempt to determine exactly who it was they were up against. They were beginning to reason for a change, instead of simply throwing away their lives and resources, waging a war they were destined to lose in any case.

So, in an effort to glimpse the inner working of the Humans, the Masters had subjected the intruders to several tests. After all, they were not really to be trifled with, having in effect defeated the Zentraedi armada.

They had even foiled the Masters own attempts to gain information about the Protoculture matrix by passive means, by accessing the information in one of the Terran master-computers, one known as EVE.

The Masters had permitted the Terrans to enter through a lower level corridor that led to the mechanical holds of the ship. It had been interesting to note they had split up their team, showing that they did indeed function independently and were not in need of a guiding intelligence. There were also demonstrations of caring and self-sacrifice, things unheard of among the Masters' race. One group was currently battling Terminators in the generator hold—the troopers were ascertaining the strength of the Humans in close-fighting techniques; another group had wandered into the Optera tree room; while a third group had found the android assembly line.

One member of the latter group had actually conversed with Musica, Mistress of the Cosmic Harp, whose songs were integral in controlling the clones of the inner centers. But that Human was now reunited with his teammates, who at the moment were returning to their predesignated rendezvous point. The second group was also en route, and so the Masters passed the thought along to the Terminators that the skirmish in the generator room be called off, allowing the third group to follow suit. Once the Humans were regrouped, the Masters would initiate a new series of challenges.

General Rolf Emerson and Colonels Anderson and Green would have given anything for a glimpse at what was going on in the fortress. But the recon team was already an hour overdue and hopes for their safe return were sliding fast. In an effort to do *something*, Emerson had ordered a stepped-up assault on the fortress, in the hope of hitting it hard enough to shake the team loose—lost ball bearings in an old fashioned pinball machine. But instead of tilting, the fortress had merely upped the ante,

filling the skies with Bioroids on their hover platforms
and sending out ground troops to combat the teams stationed at the perimeter of the crash site. It had been a
calculated gamble, but one that had not paid off.

The situation room was as busy as a hive, but the three
massive screens opposite the command balcony told a
woeful tale of defeat.

Emerson sat back into his chair to listen to the latest
sitreps from the field, none of which were encouraging. A
rescue ship sent to ATAC area thirty-four had been destroyed. Air teams were sustaining heavy casualties from
the fortress's cannon fire. Bravo Fourteen had been
wiped out completely. Sector Five had been overrun. A
rescue squad was being summoned to Bunker niner-
three-zero, where nearly a hundred men were trapped
inside. Medics were sorely needed everywhere.

"Have you reestablished communications with Lieutenant Sterling yet?" Colonel Green asked one of the
techs.

"Negative," came the reply. "But we're still trying."

Emerson caught Green's groaning sigh.

"Let's not give up on Lieutenant Sterling yet, Colonel," he told him, more harshly than was necessary. "She
won't give up until she's succeeded in her mission."

Bowie, bareheaded and precariously perched behind
and slightly above the pilot's seat of Dana's Hovertank,
tried to fill the lieutenant in on his experiences since that
elevator ride to Musica's harp chamber. He had never
been too fond of Dana's reckless road tactics, and thought
even less of them now that he had a chance to observe
things from his friend's perspective. Dana was careening
through the dark corridors at nearly top speed, not a care
in the world as she twisted the *Valkyrie* through turns its
gyrostabilizers were never meant to handle. The *Diddy-
Wa-Diddy* had been left abandoned, set on self-destruct
in the recycling hold. In an effort to take his mind off the

very real possibility of a collision, Bowie continued his rundown of the events, even though there seemed to be a lot of discrepancies in his story.

"And you say she ran away after being shot in the leg?" Dana said skeptically.

"I know it sounds incredible, but I saw it with my own eyes!" Bowie replied defensively. "And she was one beautiful lady, too," he added wistfully.

Dana threw a knowing smile over her shoulder, forcing Bowie into paroxysms of fear as she took her eyes from the corridor.

"Maybe she was an android, Bowie."

"No way."

"Then my guess is she was a dream—after all, you claim that you felt yourself being taken up into the fortress and yet we found you on the same level we entered. We didn't take any elevator rides, Bowie, and we haven't seen a stairway yet."

"But I'm telling you I went *up*, Dana! I do know up from down, you know!"

Louie went on the external speaker: "Only when you're awake, Bowie, and I don't think you were. Think back to our briefing sessions and the notes from the Gloval Expedition into the SDF-1: when the captain's team exited the dimensional fortress they were certain that hours had gone by, and yet the guards who were stationed outside the fortress swore that only fifteen minutes had elapsed!

"It could be that there is some sort of lingering effect to hyperspace travel," Louie continued unchecked, "something we're not yet aware of. Maybe time actually occurs *differently* inside the fortress than it does outside. It's something I'm going to investigate someday."

The dark hallway was suddenly opening up and filling with light, and in a moment Dana and company found themselves on a polished floor as blue as the clearest of Earth's seas—an ice-lined canal of brilliant chroma, lined with a continuous wall of turreted and arcaded buildings. Reminiscent of ancient Rome, or Florence, before the destruction visited upon it during the Global Civil War, each structure was more than two-hundred yards high, with curved, scalloped facades, ornately columned arcades crowned by friezes, and round-topped portals. Elsewhere, gracefully arched bridges crossed the solid canal, overlit by circular lights set high in the hold.

Stranger still, the hold was inhabited—by Humans.

"At least they look Human," Dana commented.

The aliens had all taken shelter under the arcades and were staring at the 15th's strange two-vehicled procession; but Dana didn't read actual fear anywhere, only an intense puzzlement, almost as though these people had no idea where they were, or what they were doing. Dress was uniformly practical, sensible, not so much fit for the Rome Dana had read about, but a Rome mock-up in the bowels of a spaceship. Shirt and trouser combinations of the same cut, the same fabric, individualized only by color or neckline, all with tight-fitting cuffs, blue, gray, gold.

Suddenly, Bowie yelled: "Lieutenant, stop the Hovertank—I just saw that girl!"

Dana and Louie cut their thrusters and the mecha settled to what seemed to be the street.

Dana wondered whether this was a show being put on for their benefit. She scanned puzzled faces in the unmoving crowds, looking for a green-haired girl.

"Are you certain it's her, Bowie?"

"I'm positive—she's one of a kind! I'd know her any —what?! It can't be! I'm seeing double!"

"Everybody here is either twins or triplets," Louie said, completing Bowie's thought. "They must be clones."

Dana followed Bowie's gaze and spied an attractive girl in chiffon, shoulder-to-shoulder with her identical twin. Clones, Dana said to herself. They had to be clones, like the Zentraedi. She thought back to what she knew of her people: how they had been grown from cell samplings of the Robotech Masters. How she herself had a part of this in her. And it suddenly occurred to her that these *clones* might very well be her sisters and brothers! Dana found herself looking around for someone who looked like her.

"Headquarters will be happy to find out that their advance intelligence reports were true," she heard Louie say.

Just then three armored shock troopers broke through the murmuring crowds, leveling laser rifles as they took up positions around the Hovertanks.

"Uh-oh—looks like we've got company!"

"Don't make a move!" one of the Terminators shouted. "We've got you covered."

"See—there's that bad movie dialogue I told you about," Bowie said.

"Cowboys and Romans," Louie muttered. "What'll we do, Lieutenant—shoot it out with them?"

"No," Dana said quickly. "If we fire into this crowd we'll end up injuring a lot of innocent people. We'll just have to try to make a break for it! Better tell your girlfriends good-bye!" she aimed at Bowie.

The Terminators opened fire as the Hovertanks lifted off, mindless of the clones their stray shots cut down.

Valkyrie and *Livewire* sped off. In the rumble seat, Bowie clung to Dana's waist, staring back at the two Musicas, heedless of the white bolts of fire snapping at the Hovertank's heels.

"Boy, this mission's a washout," Cranston was saying to Sean. "I think those jokers abandoned ship when they saw us coming."

"I'm beginning to believe you're right, Cranston," Sean admitted, absently twirling his helmet in his hand, as he slowly guided the *Bad News* away from the corridor rendezvous point. Nothing much had happened since they left the hothouse, and when neither Dana nor Dante had showed up at the designated hour, he had decided to take Cranston and Woodruff into the corridor Dana's contingent was to investigate. "I've seen more action on a Sunday School picnic," he started to say. But something was approaching them fast from up ahead, coming in from the direction of the point.

Almost before Sean could bring his weapon into ready or issue instructions to his men, Dana and Louie came tearing by them without even stopping. Sean yelled, realizing if they hadn't seen them, it wasn't likely that they would hear him. But he called out anyway, worried all of a sudden about what it was that was chasing them.

And Dana's team pulled up short.

"Wow!" Dana exclaimed. "I was beginning to think we'd never see you guys again!"

Sean was puzzled by Dana's intensity. "Yeah, well I'm happy to see you, too, Lieutenant, but I wanna tell you, this is the dullest mission I've ever been on."

"Dull?!" Dana and her team all said at once, fixing Sean with a look he couldn't quite grasp.

"Yeah. We think the aliens abandoned ship or something."

Suddenly Dana, Louie, and Bowie were all talking at him in a rush. Grant was saying something about his having been transported by an invisible elevator to the arms of a beautiful green-haired woman he had jammed with, or something. But there'd been a chase a-and that was of course why they didn't have his Hovertank with them— because they didn't chance going back to pick it up—not that they could find their way there anyway. A-and then there was this population center they had just escaped from that looked like ancient Rome and was filled with nothing but identical clones and carapace-armored shock trooper androids. . . .

When it was over all Sean could do was exchange puzzled looks with his equally perplexed teammates.

"Well, we got to see the famous forest of light-bulb trees," he told Dana. "Guess the shock troops were avoiding us for some reason."

. Just as Sean was saying this, Sergeant Dante's contingent—minus Road's Hovertank, and unfortunately, minus Road himself—hovered into view and joined them in the corridor. Dante told them of the firefight, how the aliens had crept up on them and pinned them down, only to back off unexpectedly at the last moment. . . .

He was in the middle of his explanation when the floor opened up underneath them. Nine Hovertanks and ten Humans plunged into the darkness.

"Is everybody okay? Bowie?" Dana called out into the blackness.

She knew she was wet and sticky, not from blood though, but from what she had landed in. Touching the stuff in the dark only led to more frightening images, so she groped in the opposite direction, wondering if she would stumble upon one of the Hovertanks. It would be a miracle if no one had been crushed under the falling mecha, and equally so if they all had as soft a landing as she had. There seemed to be some sort of weightlessness here—a dark and soggy lunar surface.

But one by one the teammates answered her.

"All present and accounted for. And apparently no injuries," Bowie yelled.

"Speak for yourself," Dana heard Louie say. "I've got enough bruises for the bunch of you."

"And I feel as light as a kitten in here."

"Where the heck are we, anyway?" Angelo asked. "And what's that rotten smell?"

"I've pulled enough K.P. in my time to recognize this smell anywhere," said Woodruff. "I got no idea what these aliens eat, but this is their garbage, I'll stake my wad on that."

Sean, Marino, and Xavez all made sounds of disgust.

But it was Kuri that voiced the first *uh-oh* . . .

Machinery had been activated overhead, servos were coming into play and the sound was growing louder.

"Hey . . . wait a minute," Angelo said. "This must be a freakin' *compactor*! And guess who's about to be *compacted*?!"

"I *seen* this movie, Sarge!" Xavez was suddenly moaning. "What're they tryin' to play with our heads, or what?"

"Flatten our heads is more like it!" Kuri yelled from across the blackness.

"Echo readings indicate that there is in fact a massive plate descending on us," Louie reported calmly. "I calculate forty-eight seconds until we become tomorrow morning's breakfast crepes."

Dana heard two or three of her teammates pick up handfuls of the sludge and heave it in Louie's general direction. At about the same time Louie was hit and yelled, spitting words and whatever garbage had connected with him, Dana, who had been edging forward in the darkness, hands out front like a blind person, contacted one of the Hovertanks. From the feel of it, it had landed upright, and she quickly climbed aboard and hit the lights.

It was her first mistake.

Now everyone could see the sorry state they were in. They all looked around the room, and then up at the descending plate of the compactor. Yes, it was very much like a scene from a movie they had all seen.

"Lieutenant, you gotta get us outta here!" screamed Xavez.

"Stand back, everybody. I'm gonna blast us out of here."

"You can't, Lieutenant," Louie warned her. "These

are high-density ceramic walls. They're laser resistant. I don't think it would be a good idea. If you remember that movie—"

"Then come up with a better idea, Louie. In the meantime, everybody hit the deck and hope for the best."

Hitting the deck meant diving back into the muck, but suddenly even that seemed preferable to feeling the heat of a richocheting plasma bolt.

"No-o-o!" yelled Louie once more before the end.

The bolt did just what everyone feared it would: it impacted against the wall to no effect and headed straight back from whence it came, narrowly missing Dana who ducked down into the cockpit at the last second, then caroming around the room like a homicidal billiard ball of energy, giving everyone an equal chance to dodge or be fried. Ultimately the crazed thing hit the floor of the chamber and exploded, right at the foot of Dana's mecha.

There didn't seem to be a hope that she had survived the shot. Where the Hovertank stood there was now only a huge garbage crater, smoking like a cookpot in hell. Blessedly the damn compactor had ceased its downward motion, and the hole was letting light into the room. They were all thinking that Dana had died for nothing, when suddenly they heard her voice rising from the hole. The garbage-spattered 15th grouped around the crater, peering in.

Dana was still seated in the mecha, which was now on the floor of a corridor that ran underneath the compactor. Several other Hovertanks had fallen with her, along with Xavez and Marino who were covered with grime and shaking like palsy victims.

"See—I knew it would work," Dana was saying unsteadily but knowingly. "The floor wasn't laser resistant."

No one bothered to tell her that the compactor had stopped on its own. One by one they lowered themselves through the hole, wiping off what garbage they could.

* * *

A corridor monitor blinked once and brought the reversed situation to the attention of the Masters. Things had not gone quite as planned, but the aged trio was willing to concede that no matter what happened, they were learning more about the Terrans and that was the purpose of the exercise—even though the female soldier had gotten a lucky break by finding her cannon round returned to the unprotected floor. And if anything, this only suggested that *luck* itself should be figured into the equation when dealing with this race.

The Masters next plan was to separate this most fortunate one, the apparent commander, from her team, to see how the underlings would function without her. Just how much independent thought was available to them; how resourceful were they without adequate leadership? . . .

They had managed to retrieve seven of the nine remaining Hovertanks; two were so hopelessly mired in the garbage sludge that even the mecha's thrusters couldn't break the things free—not without a good deal more time than they had to spare.

The 15th was mounted in its mecha now, Bowie still riding behind Dana, Xavez behind Marino, Woodruff behind Cranston. The sergeant, Louie, Sean, and Kuri were back in their original units.

"You sure beat the odds that time, Lieutenant," Louie commented.

Dana adjusted her helmet and made a face as she picked sticky bits of refuse from the pauldrons of her uniform. "Let's not celebrate until we're out of here," she warned all of them.

"But which way?" Louie threw to the team. "Without our helmet monitors, we can't tell one direction from another. We've gotta be down at least one level, maybe two, and unless we can find a way up I don't know how we're gonna get outta this thing."

"Dead reckoning'll get us back to that hole; I'll bet I could find my way blindfolded," the sarge announced.

"We'll just blow our way out," Dana said. "We got in: we can get out. But stay alert . . . I've got that funny feeling that we're being watched again. . . ."

No sooner had she said it than something leapt at her from the corridor ceiling. She heard Sean's warning and the rapid report of his rifle—adrenaline coursing through her like high octane—and caught the movement of the thing peripherally.

Oddly, something said to her: *snake*. And when she raised her head to look back on the thing Sean's blast had downed, she realized that that image her mind's eye conjured wasn't far from wrong: it looked like an old-fashioned wire-coiled vacuum cleaner hose, only a lot wider, and capped with an evil-looking nipplelike device. In its final moments, before Sean's second round severed the thing's tubular body, the hose loosed a massive electrical charge that narrowly missed Dana's head and exploded against the far wall of the corridor. The hose spasmed around on its ruptured neck spewing a foul-smelling smoke but no more fire.

"Good shooting, Sean!" Bowie shouted.

Louie watched the techno-assassin flail about for a moment, then glanced down at his console, noticing instantly that the radio had begun to function again. He told the team, and they realized that they must be close to the exterior wall of the fortress. There was a good chance Headquarters was monitoring them once again.

"Good," Dana said, bringing the face shield down. "Let's move out."

"Stay together this time," Sergeant Dante hastened to add.

The Masters were no longer entertained by the shenanigans of their guests, and came about as close as they could to demonstrating real emotion. And emotion made it necessary for them to break their telepathic rapport and speak directly to the Terminator. It was imperative that the Terrans not be allowed to leave the ship alive.

"See to it that all exits are sealed," said one of the Masters. "Move your sentries into corridor M-seventy-nine and use maximum force if necessary to prevent their escape.

"And see to it that Zor Prime is with your sentries," a second of the Masters thought to add, his voice betraying some ulterior motive.

Full out, the Hovertanks moved through the labyrinthine corridors of the fortress, their halogen lights piercing the darkness.

"Get ready," Dana told her teammates through the tac net. "It looks like we're going to have to fight our way out."

She hadn't actually seen anything up ahead, but as they ascended the ramp which returned them to the proper level, the mecha lamps illuminated a full line of Bioroids in the corridor ahead.

Zor Prime was leading them—the lavender-haired pilot of the red Bioroid, who had been haunting Dana's thoughts since the encounter at the Macross mounds. Diminutive against the fifty-foot high metal monsters behind him, the elfin alien was standing calmly at their fore and holding his hand up in a gesture that told the Humans to halt. When the Hovertanks accelerated instead, Zor's hand dropped decisively, a signal to his troops to open fire.

Dana tried to put the alien from her mind and called for evasive maneuvers. "Concentrate on tactical driving!"

The Bioroids opened up on the approaching Hovertanks with their disc guns, filling the corridor with white light and noise that could wake the dead. The Earth mecha weaved between hyphens of searing heat, crisscrossing in front of one another and returning fire to the wall of aliens standing between them and freedom.

Dana had a fleeting image of Zor as she swerved her Hovertank around him, unable to loose fire against him or run him over. But shortly there would be another image that would replace this last: In the dancing headlight beams the team saw two of their teammates sprawled lifeless on the corridor floor in puddles of their own blood.

Dana yelled: "It's Simon and Jordon! We can't leave them like this!"

Angelo disagreed. "It's too late to do anything for them, Lieutenant—we've got trouble up ahead."

A final Bioroid was standing guard at the exit. They certainly could have run it down without problem, but it would be a lot more profitable to take the thing alive.

Dana thought her tank through reconfiguration to Battloid. As she and Bowie rode up into the giant techno-warriors head, Dana readied herself at the controls.

"You can't take him alone," Bowie said. "He's too big!"

"He's not bigger than my Battloid," Dana reminded him. The Bioroid leapt, and Dana urged her mecha to follow. She thought the Battloid's metalshod hands into motion and grabbed the alien mecha by its pectoral armor.

Then the *Valkyrie* and its prize flew through the unmended opening. Dana didn't bother to look back.

CHAPTER
SIX

I think I breezed through the rest of the recon in a kind of trance, my thoughts so wrapped around the Eureka! *Bowie's encounter with Musica had booted up in my mind. The Masters' fortress had defolded from its hyperspace journey with particles of the Fourth Dimensional Continuum still adhering to it, iron filings to a magnet—like memory itself, alive in the Human brain despite an elapse of chronological reckoning. Immediately I set to work on a new theory based on the hypothesis that time, like light itself, was composed of quanta—packets of stuff I then called* chronons. *What I eventually arrived at—years later—was nothing so much as a reworking of Macek's turn-of-the-century theorem (then unknown to me): if you can take the time and travel, you can surely travel and take the time!*

Louie Nichols, *Tripping the Light Fantastic*

TEN OUT OF LIEUTENANT STERLING'S ORIGINAL THIR-teen had returned from the reconnaissance mission; based on the casualties sustained by the ground forces and air support who had contributed to the penetration op, this proved to be on the low side average, and Dana found some comfort there. But it wasn't the numbers that remained with her, but the sight of Privates Jordon and Simon lying on that cold floor, bathed in the harsh light from her Hovertank, their lives flowing out of them. That, and the brief moments she and Bowie and Louie had spent in the Romanesque heart of the fortress. Were those twins and triplets Human clones, or had they been fashioned from the body parts Corporal Nichols had stumbled across during the mission? Her heart told her that they were clones, brothers and sisters to the Zentraedi half of her, but Headquarters wasn't interested in her *feelings*; rightly so, they needed concrete evidence, and the sad fact was that the monitoring devices had ceased to function early on. There was, however, the Bioroid Dana's mecha had spirited from the ship, and surely the pilot of that alien craft would lay all these questions to rest; he or she wouldn't need to say a thing: it only remained to be seen whether the Earth Forces were up against androids or beings like themselves.

Dana had run these issues through her mind during the debriefing and since. Unable to sleep, she had left her bunk in the middle of the night. Sunrise found her and half the 15th in the barracks ready-room. They had all argued back and forth, unable to come to any consensus, so varied were their individual experiences inside the fortress. The squad was slated for patrol in less than an hour, and she desperately wanted to convince them that her instincts were correct.

"How can I be expected to shoot at people who might very well be my own relatives?" Dana had put to them finally. She had drawn her sidearm, and now had the distant, silent fortress bracketed in the pistol's sights. Sergeant Dante entered the room just then, and finding her thus, put a hand on her shoulder.

"I, uh, don't mean to interrupt," he said, out of real concern for the room's permaplas window.

Dana turned to dislodge his hand, and frowned as she reholstered the handgun.

"Target practice, eh? Too bad there's no aliens around to aim at."

Dana expected as much from Angelo. The mission had only served to convince him of the truth of his earlier beliefs: the aliens were nothing but bio-engineered creations that had been programmed for war. She knew that he felt the same about the Zentraedi, despite the fact that their *Humanness* had not only been proven, but was accepted by the very men and women who had once fought against them. Sean, Louie, and Bowie were acting like they weren't in the room.

"You're unbelievable, Sergeant," Dana said, disgust and disbelief in her voice. She looked to the others for support, but found none. She knew that Bowie agreed with her, especially now that he had had some sort of encounter of his own inside the ship, but he was too timid to make a stand. The vote was still out on Louie: like the staff at HQ, he was going to need clearcut evidence before saying anything. Sean, as always, had no opinion one way or another.

"I suppose you think we should shoot every alien on sight, huh? Would that make you happy?"

Angelo smirked. It was so easy to get to her. But that wasn't really his purpose; he merely wanted to get to the Human side of her. "Well, we'd be a lot safer, Lieutenant. And I don't think anybody on their side's gonna hesitate to fire at us."

Angelo had turned his back to her and was walking away, when a messenger entered unannounced through the room's sliding doors.

"Sir," the aide said stiffly, offering his salute. "General Emerson requests your presence. I'm to escort you and Corporal Nichols to Dr. Beckett's lab immediately."

Dana told the messenger to wait outside. She turned temporary command of the team over to Sergeant Dante, feeling as though she had lost a minor battle.

The Robotech Masters felt the same.

The three had summoned their Scientist and Politician triumvirates to the fortress command nexus after the Earthlings had made their daring escape.

"I expect a full report on damage to our ship and an update on the Micronian position," said the Master called Bowkaz. "Micronian" was a term the Masters used when speaking to any of their numerous clones, a holdover from Zentraedi times.

There was an unmistakable note of desperation in his voice, a fact that at once distressed and pleased the three Scientist clones—androgynous figures, with exotic features and long hair in brilliant colors.

"Most of the damage is isolated to the Reflex power modules," reported the honey-haired Scientist. "The Micronians will probably attack again. We should escalate our combat profile."

"How could the situation have come to this?" Dag asked rhetorically. Like his companion Masters he was hawk-nosed and liquid-eyed, monkish looking in the long gown whose triple collars mimicked the Flower of Life's tripartite structure. "It was never our intention to destroy the Micronians or their planet."

One of the young Politicians spoke to that. He resembled the Scientists in form and figure, save for the fact that he was dressed in togalike wrappings, and of course had been bio-engineered for political rather than scientific functions.

"The Micronians feel threatened by our presence here," he reminded the Masters now.

"But they must realize that our clones are not here to tamper with their civilization," said Shaizan, who was in many ways the Masters' true spokesman, most often called upon to communicate directly with the Elders of Tirol. "The true threat to both our races is the parasitic Invid, who will themselves come in search of the Protoculture."

Which was and was not true; but the Masters were compelled to make their clones feel that the journey to Earth was more noble than it actually was.

"We must complete our mission before the Invid arrive," Bowkaz countered. "The Micronians are dangerous and must be destroyed if they continue to obstruct us."

"I agree," Dag said after a moment of reflection. "The

Micronian ignorance of our purpose and their inexperience with the Protoculture makes them a dangerous threat to our cause."

"And too many of our own Bioroid pilots have been severely injured to mount an effective attack against them at this time," Bowkaz hastened to add.

"Are our shields holding?" Shaizan asked of the Scientists.

Schematic representations of the fortress's energy system capabilities came to life on the oval-shaped screen that filled the interstices of the command center's neural-like structure.

"We estimate a functional capacity of only twenty percent," returned one of the Scientists. "Not even powerful enough to seal breaches in the fortress's hull."

"If we cannot leave and we cannot fight, then what option is left us?" asked a second.

The three Politicians and the three Scientists waited for the Master's pronouncements. Ultimately it was Shaizan who answered them.

"We must use the Micronians," he said somewhat haltingly. "First we will take some of their kind and subject them to a xylonic cerebral probe to determine whether or not we can turn them into Bioroid pilots. This will serve a dual purpose: first, it will allow us to strengthen our forces. Second, by allowing one of these reengineered pilots to be captured, we will be able to convince the Micronians that they have been manipulated into fighting their own kind. This will buy us the time we need to effect repairs or call in a rescue ship. In the meantime, we must reformulate our thinking and come up with a plan to secure the Protoculture matrix before it is too late."

The partially-dissected shell of the captured alien Bioroid lay on its back on a massive platform in Dr. Beckett's Defense Center laboratory. Colonels Anderson and Green, along with several forensic engineers and computer techs, were already in attendance when General Emerson entered with Dana and Louie in tow.

"I think you're going to find this very interesting," Beckett said by way of introduction.

He was a nondescript-looking man in his late thirties, with thick, amber-tinted glasses and a crisply starched white uniform he kept tightly fastened at neck and cuffs. Known for the yard-long pointer he was said to carry wherever he went, Beckett had little of Professor Cochran's savvy, and nowhere near the intellectual power of someone like Zand; but he was competent enough, and Louie Nichols let him ramble on for several minutes before saying anything.

"Let me start by saying that this thing is a complicated network of mechanical parts controlled by biological stimuli, the origin of which is uncertain at this time." Beckett used his pointer to indicate a control panel located below and to the left of the Bioroid's head. "However, we think that this module here acts as a sensor device, or overload circuit mechanism." He gave the panel several taps with the pointer.

"Then if you bypass that relay," Louie interjected, reaching for one of the Bioroid's sensor cables and coiling it around his forearm, " . . . ah, these should act like some sort of muscle."

Dana, who was standing next to the corporal, watched the arm of the Bioroid begin to twitch as Louie flexed the muscles in his forearm. Startled, she stepped back from the platform, worried that the thing was going to attack.

"Don't worry, Lieutenant," Louie said, full of confidence. "It's not going anywhere." He gestured to his forearm and once again flexed; the Bioroid's arm gave another shudder. "It's only responding to the stimulus I'm giving it."

"Like power-amplified body armor," Dana said, relaxing some.

"Bingo," said Louie, taking off his wrappings.

Emerson, Green, and Anderson looked to Beckett to elaborate. The doctor cleared his throat and said: "Yes . . . In many ways it functions rather like our own Veritechs, only in place of our sensor gloves and helmets, it seems to be directly attuned to its pilot."

Beckett instructed one of his techs to project the data he had prepared for the preliminary report. All eyes turned to the wallscreen above the forensic platform. Various schematic representations and readouts of the Bioroid's systems filled the screen as the Doctor spoke.

"It is indeed a type of armored suit that responds to the stimuli provided by a pilot. Through a complex network of bio-mechanical diodes, it actually interfaces with its pilot and carries out the pilot's commands in a matter of nanoseconds." Beckett paused as a new schematic assembled itself. "The difference here is that the pilot, too, seems to have been bio-engineered to interface with the mecha."

"So that's why they're so maneuverable," Dana said.

"Then this Bioroid is an extension of its pilot?" asked the bearded Green, still unsure what Beckett and this young corporal with the dark goggles were getting at.

"Exactly," the doctor said. "The circuits of the one *duplicate* the circuits of the other. We have yet to determine how such an imprint has been made possible, but there is no mistaking the accomplishment."

"But this is incredible," Emerson said. "You're suggesting a bio-mechanical lifeform."

Beckett shook his head. "A pilot *is* required," he started to say before Colonel Green broke in.

"What's the most effective way to stop these things once and for all?" the colonel demanded.

Dana, meanwhile, now had the cable wrapped around her own arm. If the Bioroid required a living pilot, then her case for the *Humanness* of the aliens was made. It would have been redundant to put *androids* in the bioroids' cockpits. . . .

She tuned in for Beckett's response to Green's query, holding her tongue until the right moment. The doctor was once again tapping his pointer on the Bioroid's neck module.

"Well, considering what we now know about the design, I'd say the most effective shot would have to be placed in the area of this control mechanism."

Rolf Emerson now stepped forward, as if to silence everyone. "I'd like to have your input, Lieutenant Sterling. You and your team have engaged these things hand-to-hand, as it were. Did either of you observe any weak points in their individual defense systems?"

Dana shrugged. "I was too wrapped up in tactics to notice anything."

"Is the Bioroid equipped with any kind of micro-recorder?" Louie asked Dr. Beckett. "Because if it is," he went on without waiting for a reply, "there must be some sort of internal damage-control monitoring system.... Our main computer could access the data and—"

"We've already seen to that, Corporal," Beckett interrupted, noticeably peeved. "Display the pertinent data," he said to the tech at the console.

"I think I know why these things have been so hard to stop," Louie muttered to Dana as new schematics scrolled across the wallscreen. "Display the damaged sections individually," he instructed the computer tech, stealing Beckett's thunder.

Louie stepped up to the screen and ran through an explanation of the data for General Emerson and the other brass, but it was Beckett who said: "The Bioroids are unaffected by direct hits unless you can destroy the cockpit."

"That's the way I read it," Louie seconded, no trace of competition in his voice.

"All right," said a pleased Colonel Anderson. "I'll make it a standing order to aim only at the cockpit."

It was the moment Dana had been worried about, the

order she feared. "You can't do that, Colonel!" she blurted out, surprising all of them. "You'll be destroying the pilots as well as the Bioroids!"

Anderson seemed slightly bemused by the outburst. "Well I think that should be obvious, Lieutenant. The android pilot would be destroyed along with his machine. . . ."

"But they're *not* androids! It would make for a redundant system," she said, looking to Louie for help. She made mention of their experiences in the ship, the city of clones.

Green made a dismissive gesture. "But you have no proof that those, ah, *people* weren't simply androids. What about this android assembly line you claimed to have seen—"

"Exactly what do we know about the captured pilot?" Emerson asked Beckett. The doctor made a wry face and looked over to Green, who fielded the question, red-faced.

"I'm sorry to report that the pilot sustained some serious injuries as a result of our rather hasty efforts to remove it from the Bioroid. However, our medical teams are doing everything possible. . . ."

Green let his words trail off as a messenger entered the lab.

"General Emerson, your presence is requested in the war room. Commander Leonard is receiving a briefing on the captured alien pilot."

"How is the pilot?" Emerson asked.

Eyes-front, the messenger replied: "It stopped functioning over an hour ago, Sir. But the autopsy is complete."

General Emerson asked Dana to accompany him to the war room; it was the first time they had had a chance to talk in some weeks, but Rolf was careful to steer the conversation away from the issue of the aliens. He knew

full well what must be going through Dana's mind, but
there was as yet no proof about the nature or identity of
the invaders. Rolf hoped that the briefing would put an
end to this once and for all, and wondered what Dana's
mother would have done. But then, had Admiral Hunter,
Max, Miriya, and the others, not gone off on their Expeditionary Mission, none of this might be happening now.
Miriya had turned against her own kind once before, and
Rolf was certain that she would have remained on Earth's
side in the present conflict.

Dana had to be made to realize that the Zentraedi
were in no way connected with the Robotech Masters. Of
course it was true that as clones of that very group there
was blood between them, but the Zentraedi had gone off
on their own; they had become their own people, and
Dana was more than any other Zentraedi representative
of this great change. There was no kinship between her
and these clones the Robotech Masters had brought to
Earth; there was only enmity between them; she had no
brothers or sisters to that ship, any more than the people
of Earth who had fought one another through the course
of history felt blood between themselves.

The chiefs-of-staff were seated around that grouping of
tables Rolf still wished triangular, with Leonard in his
customary place at the curved apex, and Dr. Byron from
Defense Medical standing off to his right. Byron was a
tall man, whose head often appeared too small for his
massive torso. He had sharp, pointed features, and a dark
brown mustache that was a perfect inverted match for his
arched and bushy eyebrows, giving his face a somewhat
comic turn, at odds with the no nonsense forcefulness of
his personality.

Emerson and Sterling's entry had obviously interrupted the man. Rolf introduced Dana to Leonard and
the staff, seeing the analytical glint in the supreme commander's eye now that he had a visual image of this person he had not seen in years, save for a brief handshake

at the Academy ceremonies. But he was more than civil to Dana, complimenting her on the recon mission and the capture of the Bioroid.

Leonard bade Dr. Byron continue with his findings.

"First of all, we found something remarkable inside the pilot's body," Byron said, reading from his notes. "There was some sort of bio-electrical device implanted in its solar plexus. Subsequent analysis of this showed it to be similar to the animating chips used early on by Dr. Emil Lang's teams of Robotechnicians in the manufacture of Earth mecha."

Emerson's hand shot up. He gestured impatiently until Byron acknowledged him.

"I'm sorry to interrupt, Doctor. But was the pilot human or not?"

"Oh, definitely not human," Byron said, shaking his head.

Rolf heard Dana's heavy sigh of disappointment as the doctor continued.

"But I will say that it surpasses anything we ever attempted in the way of bio-mechanical creations. In fact, this animating device we found in the android's solar plexus is nothing if not akin to an artificial soul."

The supreme commander cleared his throat loudly. "Let's keep theology out of this," he directed at Byron. "Just stick to the facts, Doctor."

Byron winced at the rebuke and nervously adjusted the collar of his jacket.

"Our belief is that this race was forced to adapt to hostile environments as it began its expansion across the galaxy, and that an android bio-system was the natural outgrowth of this."

Leonard broke in again. "These aliens are not even the micronized Zentraedi we first thought, but an army of programmed androids in control of devastating bio-mechanical weapons. It's obvious to me that the Robotech Masters found it much easier to use androids than clones." He looked around the tables, then stood up, hands pressed to the table. "So much the easier for us, then. We are waging a war against an artificial lifeform, gentlemen, and we should have no qualms about destroying it—*utterly*."

Suddenly Dana was on her feet. "Commander, you're mistaken," she said. She raised her voice a notch to cut through the comments. "That Bioroid ·pilot may have been an android, but I believe that we're dealing with a race of living beings—not a soulless army of machines."

Byron narrowed his eyes and rocked forward on the balls of his feet. "My observations are completely documented," he countered. "What proof do you have to back up this absurd position?"

"I've had some first-hand experience in dealing with them," Dana shot back. But she now felt Rolf's hand tighten on her arm.

"Sterling, sit down!" he told her.

Leonard looked furious. "Look here, I'm familiar with your report, but it's possible you've misread your experiences, Lieutenant. The aliens could have implanted certain things in your mind. If they're capable of creating androids of this advanced form, who knows what else they're able to do?"

"No," Dana said back to him. "Why do you refuse to accept the possibility I might be right?!"

Leonard slammed his fist on the table. "Don't provoke us, Lieutenant. Quiet down at once or I'll be forced to have you removed from this session."

But Dana was on a roll, the persistent nature of her alien side well in control of her now. "You're fools if you refuse to hear me out!" she told the staff.

"Remove this insubordinate!" Leonard commanded. "I've heard enough!"

Two sentries had stepped in and taken hold of her arms.

But Emerson, too, was on his feet now. "Perhaps we should listen to her."

"I haven't got time for her disruptions," Leonard said stiffly.

Dana was pulled from the room, twisting and kicking, even breaking free of their hold once to call everyone an idiot. Rolf only hoped that Leonard was willing to overlook some of it. He sat down as a conciliatory gesture, exchanging looks with the supreme commander.

"Go on with your report, Dr. Byron," Leonard said after a moment.

Byron wrapped things up, losing most of the staff when he turned to technicalities.

Leonard cleared his throat.

"Gentlemen, it seems to me our course is clear: we must commit ourselves to the total destruction of these androids."

All but Emerson voiced their concurrence.

Leonard threw the chief of staff a dirty look as he stood up. "Do you have something to add, General?"

Emerson kept his voice controlled. "Only this: if these aliens possess any human qualities, we should try to negotiate. Fighting can't be the only alternative. Look what happened during the Robotech War—"

"Surely you don't believe that we could ever come to terms with a group of barbarians, do you Emerson?"

"That's probably just what Russo and Hayes and the rest of the UEDC said before Dolza's armada incinerated this planet," Rolf said with a sneer. "I believe *anything* is better than a continued loss of lives."

"Perhaps, perhaps," the supreme commander allowed. "But their advanced technology leaves us no other choice. Even if we *could* negotiate, we'd be doing so from a position of weakness, not strength, and that could prove fatal. It's out of the question! Now, will there be anything else from you, *General*?"

Leonard hadn't even heard him, Rolf said to himself as

he took his seat. Worse, the commander was actually repeating the justification Russo and his doomed council had used before firing the Grand Cannon at an alien armada of over four million warships.

"No, Commander," Emerson said weakly. "Not now."

Someone will whisper the proper words over our graves.

CHAPTER
SEVEN

Confronted with the issue of [Supreme Commander Leonard's] militaristic megalomania, we are tempted to point to the past and remind one another that history repeats itself. I know of no other statement that so demeans us as a planetary race. Since Humankind looked the Monolith in the face this authorless theory has been used to both excuse and justify our shortsightedness and shortcomings; to explain away our foolish actions and violent choices. But isn't it time that we asked ourselves why history has to repeat itself? Short of positing a new theory of reincarnation—with the same greedy men caught up in an eternal return to wage the same war over and over again—we are left in the dark. Certainly Leonard was being pressured by Chairman Moran, and certainly he had inherited the bloodstained mantle left behind by T. R. Edwards; but where are the actual chains, biogenetic or otherwise, that enslave him to history's dark flow? Perhaps we should look to the Robotech Masters for answers. Or the Protoculture itself.

Major Alice Harper Argus (ret.), *Fulcrum: Commentaries on the Second Robotech War*

"THE OFFICERS ON THE GENERAL STAFF ARE nothing but a bunch of idiots," Dana reported to her teammates when she rejoined them in Monument Sector Five, a usually crowded downtown district of shopping and office malls that was all but deserted today.

With Angelo Dante in temporary command, the squad had just relieved the 14th squad Tactical Armored and already positioned their Hovertanks. Dana had roared up out of nowhere, executing a neat front leap from the nose of the *Valkyrie*, and immediately begun to regale them with an account of the briefing session with Commander Leonard. Both Sean and Angelo wondered to themselves what might be the outcome of Dana's being forcibly ejected from the war room; either one of them stood the chance of receiving a promotion if the lieutenant was busted because of her actions.

Louie waited for Dana to finish before telling her what he had learned at the forensic lab after she had left.

"We discovered that the relay we thought was a control device is actually some kind of sonic frequency receiver."

"So?" Dana asked him.

Louie adjusted his goggles. "So the Bioroid is probably controlled by a mixture of telepathic suggestion and signals from artificial sensors.'

Dana's face fell. "You mean the Bioroids aren't controlled by the pilots? After I just shot off my mouth back there—"

"I'm sure they *can* be," Louie said encouragingly, "but not like we originally thought. It looks like some kind of higher intelligence may be controlling them by remote control."

"I don't get it," said Angelo, trying to scratch his head through his helmet.

"Someone or something is actually feeding instructions to the android pilots," Louie explained.

"They're not clones then?"

Louie shook his head.

Dana still refused to believe any of this. "Well, anyway," she started to say, "I told them. . . ."

All at once alert sirens were blaring throughout the city. Dana ordered everyone back to their Hovertanks (executing yet a second gymnastic leap as she mounted her own), and switched on her radio. The net was alive with a thousand voices, but she didn't need to try and make sense of the reports. One look up explained everything: the skies above Monument City were filled with the aliens' scarablike troop carriers.

"It's a full-scale enemy attack!" Sean said.

"If you have any alternative, don't shoot directly at their cockpits," Louie yelled before he threw himself into the Hovertank's seat. "We might be able to capture one!"

Hundreds of alien ships were closing on the city, but now, even higher overhead, appeared the telltale atmospheric streaks of Alpha fighters, breaking formation and falling in to engage their Robotech enemies. A hail of brilliant yellow fire, calculated to angle away from the city itself, was launched against the invaders, Skylord and Swordfish missiles and Teflon rounds impacting on the rust-colored crafts' armored hulls to little or no effect. The sky was lit up with tracers, dazzling crescents of light, and fiery explosions. But the troop carriers continued their attack, not only weathering the storm, but returning their own brand of hell fire as the Alphas completed their descent and dropped below them. The four-muzzled guns of revolving undercarriage turrets spewed light and death across the sky, taking down fighters faster than the eye could keep track. Trailing tails of dense black smoke, Alphas plunged uncontrolled toward the city, while others were simply disintegrated in midflight. Pilots drifting homeward on synsilk chutes were cut down as well.

"It looks like there's more than we can handle, Lieutenant," Angelo shouted over the net.

Dana said nothing. There had to be a way to disable those Bioroids without harming the pilots, she thought. There had to be a way—but *how*?

Now hatches on the side of the troop carriers sprang open. Bioroids mounted on their Hoverplatforms were disgorged from the ships in a seemingly unending line. They fell upon the city, untouched by the Alpha fighters, outmaneuvering them in almost every instance and bringing their own disc guns to bear against them. The Bioroids fanned out over the city, as though searching for something that had as yet eluded them. From every sector came reports of their descent, but there was no clearcut sense of their motive. They landed finally in unvarying groups of three and spread through the city streets on foot.

Most of Monument City was packed away in the enormous underground shelters that had become as much a part of city life since the Global Civil War as a Sunday stroll in the park. But, as always, there were those who had opted to return home first to salvage some precious knickknack, or make certain that family or friends had already departed; and then there were the diehards who simply refused, and the thrill-seekers who lived for this sort of thing. And it was these last groups that the Bioroids moved against, fulfilling the directives of the Masters to capture as many Micronians as possible. Unseen by Dana and the rest of the 15th, and as yet unreported by the Civil Defense networks, the Bioroids were engaged in a novel form of looting: using their massive metalshod fists to smash through the walls of dwellings and shops, and grab in those same hands whatever Human stragglers they could find, often unknowingly crushing them to death before returning them to the troop carriers.

Ultimately the Bioroids entered the canyons of downtown and found the 15th waiting for them.

Sean said, "Heads up, folks, here they come!"

"Have any bright ideas, Louie?" the sarge asked.

"Yeah, I do," the corporal answered, ignoring Dante's sarcasm. "If you aim to either side of the cockpit, you can temporarily paralyze the pilot."

"Now why the hell would I want to do that, Nichols?!" Dante bellowed.

Dana cut into the tac net. "Angelo, just do as he says —it's important," she announced cryptically. "We've got to try to avoid hitting the pilots directly."

"Whose side are you on?" Dante got out just in time.

The Bioroids loosed plasma bolts from their Hoverplatforms top-mounted guns as they approached, one of the first shots finding Dante's mecha; the explosion threw the Hovertank fifty feet from its position in the center of the street, but the sergeant rode it out, reconfiguring to Gladiator mode during the resultant back flip and swinging the cannon around for a counterstrike. Dana had also reconfigured her mecha. She hopped the self-propelled gun over to Dante's new resting place, just as the sergeant blew one of the Bioroids from the air.

"Angelo, listen to me—I want you to try to shoot down their Hovercraft first."

"What are you up to, Lieutenant?" he fired back at her.

"Once you've got 'em off their Hovercraft," Dana went on, "shoot at their legs and put 'em out of commission." She was trying her best to make this sound appealing to Dante, but she could just imagine his face, screwed up in anger under the helmet.

The Bioroids were coming in low now, not more than ten yards off the ground, Bowie, Sean, and Louie a barricade they'd never get past. The 15th trio blew the Hoverplatforms out from under the attackers, even as explosions rocked the street all around them. Bioroids fell with ground-shaking crashes, while others decided to leap from their crafts and take up positions in recessed doorways and storefronts. Downtown became a war zone as both sides pumped pulsed fire through the streets. The sides of highrise buildings collapsed and cornices and friezes crumbled to the cratered street. Glass rained down in deadly slivers from windows blown out high above the fighting.

Dana ordered her team to reconfigure from Gladiator to Battloid for possible hand-to-hand encounters.

The street and surrounding area was pure devastation now, but the enemy had been held at the 15th's line. No one bothered to ask what the aliens were looking for, or where they hoped to get. Still in Battloid mode, the squad headed for the cover and continued to trade salvos with the entrenched group who had taken the far end of the avenue. Once again, Dana reminded them to go for the legs and not the cockpits. But this time Sean took issue with her.

"They can still blast us if we do that," he pointed out. "We've gotta take a chance and aim at an area near those cockpits, Lieutenant."

"They're androids, damn it, *androids*!" Angelo yelled over the net.

"I'm convinced they're *not*, Sergeant!"

"Well what's the difference whether they're androids or clones?!" Dante said as debris from a shattered store sign fell on him. He thought his Battloid through a front leap that took him clear across the street. "They're still *shooting* at us!"

"We've got to capture one!"

Without warning, a Bioroid appeared behind Dana's mecha and loosed a blast at her. She spun but not in time. Fortunately Angelo saw the move and managed to take the thing out, slugs from his chaingun tearing open the enemy's cockpit.

"So much for leg shots," Dante said.

"That's one I owe you," Dana responded tight-lipped.

Bioroids had taken to the rooftops and were pouring everything they had into the street. Troop carriers were dropping in to assist, and things quickly took a turn for the worse.

"We'll never be able to hold them!" Sean said, voicing what all of them were thinking.

But just as suddenly, the battle began to reverse itself, through no effort of the 15th. The Bioroids were returning to their Hoverplatforms and making for the scarab ships, seemingly in retreat.

Dante said as much over the net and ranged in the *Trojan Horse*'s forward viewfinder. One of the Bioroids had a civilian clutched in its hand. Dante turned and found another—the civilian limp, probably dead. Everywhere he looked now, he saw the same scene.

"They're taking hostages!" he told Dana. Traversing his cannon, he took aim on one of the Bioroids, muttering to himself, "You're a goner now, buddy. . . ."

But Dana positioned her Battloid in front of him, preventing a clear shot at his target.

"Angelo, stop! You'll kill the hostage—"

Two Bioroids blew the words from her, with shots that would have thrown her face-forward to the ground had Dante not been there to catch her.

"That's *two* I owe you," she said with some effort.

They both dropped their Battloids into a crouch and returned fire. Many of the Bioroids were left without Hovercraft and were obviously bent on going down fighting. There would be no captives here, just a scrap pile of mecha and android parts.

Dana did manage to blow the legs out from under one of their number, but a second later the thing seemed to self-destruct. And when they did that, there weren't even *parts* left, just memories.

Further down the street the troop carriers were lifting off. The 15th was pinned down, unable to stop them. Still other carriers were landing close in to the fighting, picking up troops who would have been abandoned. *Could they be getting short of firepower*, Dana wondered?

The 15th pushed their line forward and took two more city blocks from the dwindling number of enemy troops. Then ultimately they found themselves firing on the carriers themselves as they were lifting off, presumably returning to the fortress.

"There they go," Dante said, laying his weapon aside. "I wonder what they're planning to do with all those hostages?"

"That's a good question, Sergeant," said Bowie.

"Yeah, a *real* good question," said Sean.

General Emerson and Commander Leonard watched the withdrawal from the central tower of the command center. Below, much of the city was in ruin; the sky above was smoke and orange flame.

"Negotiating couldn't have been worse than this!" Emerson said in disgust, turning away from the window.

"Don't make assumptions," Leonard told him from his seat. "Who's to say that if we had tried to sit down and reason with them the results would have been any different? We may have prevented a worse disaster."

Emerson was too frustrated to counter the remark.

A staff officer entered the room just then and Leonard got to his feet anxiously.

"Well, what's the figure?" he demanded.

"Over two hundred citizens have been kidnapped, sir. But the figure may go higher once all sectors have reported in."

"I see...." Leonard said, visibly distressed. "In the official report, list them as casualties of the battle."

Emerson threw Leonard a look, which the commander took in stride. *Did the fool really expect him to tell the civilian population that the aliens were now taking people from their homes for some unknown purpose?*

"Yessir," the staff sergeant snapped.

"I don't know what they're up to," Leonard said under his breath. "But whatever it is, it won't work—not as long as I have a single man left to fight them."

CHAPTER
EIGHT

Come on, people, we've done this before and we can do it again. There isn't one of us—except for the tots—who didn't see our homes and lives wiped out by the rounds and missiles of one faction or another. So, think back to those days, remember how we had to build and rebuild. And remember that we never lost sight of tomorrow. We can lean on each other and pull through this, or we can all retreat into our individual misery and lose everything. I'm going to leave it up to each and every one of you. But I know what I'm going to do: I'm going to roll up my shirtsleeves, grab hold of this shovel, and dig myself out of this mess!

From Mayor Tommy Luan's speech to the residents of SDF-1 Macross, as quoted in Luan's *High Office*

THE HUMAN BOOTY THAT RESULTED FROM THE Bioroid raid on Monument City was being housed in a massive stasis sphere inside the Masters' grounded flagship—a luminescent globe over fifty yards in diameter that had once been used to store the specimen clones derived from the cell tissues of the Tirolian scientist, Zor. Of the three-hundred-odd victims of the kidnapping foray, only seventy-five had survived the ordeal. These men, women, and children were drifting weightlessly in the gaseous chamber now, as the three Masters looked on dispassionately. The time had come to subject one of the captives to a xylonic cerebral probe to determine not only the psychological make-up of the Humans, but to ascertain their involvement with the Protoculture as well.

At the Masters' behest an antigrav beam retrieved one

of the deanimated Earthling males and conveyed him to the mind probe table, a circular platform something like a light table, lit up by the internal circuitry of its numerous scanning devices. The subject was a young tech, still in uniform, his handsome face a mask of death. He was carefully positioned supine on the transparent surface of the platform by the antigrav beam, while the Masters took to the table's control console, a bowllike apparatus slightly larger than the xylonic scanner, its rim a series of pressure-sensitive activation pads.

"But can we extract the information we want from what is no doubt an inferior example of the species?" Bowkaz put to his companions. Their choice had been based on the fact that this one was clothed in an Earth Forces uniform; there had been captives of higher rank, but they had expired in transit.

"We will at least be able to determine the depth of their reliance on the Protoculture," Dag returned.

Six wrinkled hands were laid on the sensor pads; the combined will of three minds directed the scanning process. X-ray images and internal schematics of the Human were displayed on the control console's central screen.

"Their evolutionary development is more limited than we thought," Shaizan commented.

As the probes were focused on cerebral memory centers, video images replaced the roller-coaster graphics; these so-called mnemonic schematics actually translated the electroengrammic cerebral pulses into visual wavelengths, permitting the Masters to view the subject's past. What played on the circular monitor screen were scenes that were to some extent archetypically human· preverbal memories of infancy, recollections of school life, cadet training, moments of love and loss, beauty and pain.

The Masters had little trouble understanding the images of training and hierarchical induction, but were less certain when the scenes contained some measure of emotional content.

"Inefficient command structure and grotesquely primitive weapons system," Bowkaz offered, as military memories surfaced.

Now a fleeting image of a run through Earth's tall green grass, a companion alongside . . .

"Is this the specimen's female counterpart?"

"Most likely. Our previous studies have shown that the two sexes intermix quite freely and that the Earthlings apparently select specific mates. I believe that we are seeing an example of what might be referred to as the courting ritual."

"A barbaric behavioral pattern."

"Yes . . . The species reproduces itself through a process of self-contained childbirth. There is no evidence of biogenetic engineering whatsoever."

"Random . . . foolish," muttered Dag.

"But something about them is worrisome," said Shaizan. "It is no wonder the Zentraedi were defeated." He lifted his aged hands from the sensor pads, effectively deactivating the probe.

The young cadet on the table sat up, seemingly unaffected and reawakened; but there was no life left in his eyes: whatever was once his individual self had been taken from him by the Masters' probe, and what remained was empty consciousness, like a hand wiped clean of prints and lines, awaiting that first fold and flex. . . .

"There is little chance of using these beings to pilot our Bioroids," Bowkaz pronounced. "The scanning process alone has destroyed much of this one's neural circuitry. We would need to recondition each of them to suit our purpose. . . ."

But if this part of their plan was foiled, it was at least encouraging to have learned that not all Humans had knowledge of the Protoculture, except in terms of its application to the enhancement of technology. They had not yet discovered its true value. . . .

". . . And this is to our advantage," said Dag. "Ignorant, they will not oppose our removing the Protoculture matrix from the ruins of Zor's dimensional fortress."

"But we must prevent them from carrying out these attacks against us. Can they be reasoned with?"

Bowkaz scowled. "They can be threatened."

"And easily manipulated . . . I feel that the time has come to call down a rescue ship."

"But we are so close to our goal," Dag objected.

Shaizan looked to his companion. There was an unmistakable element of impatience in Dag's attitude, surely a contagion spread by the Earthlings who had been allowed to scout the fortress. Or perhaps by the very specimens the Bioroids had brought in. All the more reason to abandon the surface of the planet as quickly as possible.

"The time has come for us to activate Zor Prime and insinuate him among the Humans. The clone so resembles them that they will accept him as one of their own."

Bowkaz concurred. "We will achieve a two-fold purpose: by implanting a neuro-sensor in the clone's brain, we will be able to monitor and control his activities."

"And second?" Dag asked anxiously.

"The realization of our original plan for the clone: as the contamination takes hold of him, the neural imagery of Zor will be awakened. And once that occurs, we will not only know precisely where the Protoculture device has been hidden, but exactly how it operates."

Shaizan came close to smiling. "The Invid will be stopped and the galaxy will be *ours* once again."

Bowkaz looked at the Human subject, then the stasis sphere itself. "And what of these?" he asked his companions.

Shaizan turned his back. "Destroy them," he said.

"Specimen is in position and proton disposal is on standby," reported the bio-lab tech.

Commander Leonard stepped to the permaplas observation window and gave a last look at the alien android.

It had been laid out on its back on a flyout platform central to the huge sanitization tank. Curiously, someone in forensic had thought to reclothe the dissected thing in its uniform. Consequently, this routine disposal was beginning to feel more like a wake than anything else, and Leonard didn't like that one bit.

The sanitization chamber resembled the sealed barrel of an enormous gun, its curved inner surface an array of circular ports linked by conduits to tanks of cleansing chemicals or particle-beam accelerators. No one had expected the supreme commander to drop by, and it was only happenstance that accounted for his presence—he and his retinue had been in the area and Colonel Fredericks of the GMP had invited him over to witness the process. Rolf Emerson was also present.

Leonard was just about ready to give the tech the go-sign, when Lieutenant Sterling came running in, urging him to wait, urging him not to give the signal.

"Commander," she said out of breath. "You can't just destroy him. He should be returned to his people. Perhaps we can bargain—"

Leonard was still burning from Dana's interruptions at the briefing, so he turned on her harshly now, gesturing to the lifeless form in the tank. "It's an unthinking piece of protoplasm even when alive, *Lieutenant*! Do you seriously believe that the aliens would bargain for *this*?!"

Rolf Emerson was ready to drag Dana away before she could respond, but she ignored his glare, even raised her voice some. "Why would 'unthinking pieces of protoplasm' bother to take Human hostages, Commander? Answer that!"

Leonard winced and looked around, wondering if anyone without a clearance had caught Sterling's comment. Fredericks understood, and stepped behind Dana, gently taking hold of her arms.

"Let me go!" Dana threw over her shoulder.

Fredericks backed off, then said in low tones: "Calm

down, Lieutenant. There were no hostages taken yesterday, there were only casualties. And in any event, this matter has nothing whatever to do with you."

"Activate!" Dana heard the commander say. He had turned away from her, hands folded behind his back, silhouetted against the observation window now as a flash of bright light disintegrated the alien corpse. Follow-up chemicals poured from two ports removing any remaining traces of tissue.

Dana stood motionless; unresponsive to Leonard as he shouldered by her, dismissing her. Fredericks and Emerson closed in on her.

"Now then, Lieutenant," the GMP colonel began sinisterly.

"Will you take your hands *off* me?!" Dana yelled, twisting free of his grip.

Rolf stepped in front of her. "Dana," he said, controlled but obviously furious, "considering your past record, you risk a great deal by coming here like this. You know the punishment for insubordination is severe—and don't think for a moment that I'll intervene on your behalf."

"Yes, of course. Sir!"

Rolf softened some. "Believe me, I share your concern that Commander Leonard has been too resolute in this matter, but I'm in no position to debate his actions and neither are *you*. Do I make myself clear?"

Dana's lips were a thin line. "Clear, sir," she said stiffly. "Clear as day."

The 15th, like many of the other ATAC squads, had been assigned to mop-up duty. There were sections of Monument City untouched by the recent attack, but this was more than made up for by the devastation elsewhere. Still, it was business as usual for the civilians: thanks to Robotechnology, rebuilding wasn't the chore it would have been twenty years ago, even though there were relatively few mecha units given over to construction. Many wondered how Macross had been able to rebuild itself so often without the advantage of modern techniques and materials, not to mention modular design innovations. One would hear stories about Macross constantly, comparisons and such, but what always surfaced was a sense of nostalgia for the older, cruder ways, nostalgia for a certain *spirit* that had been lost.

Dana's generation didn't quite see things that way, however. In fact, they felt that Monument had *more* spirit than any of its prototypes. Whereas Hunter's generation had been brought up during an era of war—the Civil War, then the Robotech—Dana and her peers had enjoyed almost twenty years of peace. But they had been raised to *expect* war, and now that it was here, they simply did their part, then returned to the hedonistic pursuits that had always ruled them and provided them with a necessary balance to the dark predictions of their parents and elders.

In this way, mop-up operations were usually excuses for block parties. Civilians left the shelters and started partying as soon as they could, and the younger members of the Army of the Southern Cross were so easily distracted and seduced. . . .

"Get a move on, Bowie!" Dana yelled over her shoulder, as she leaned her Hovercycle into a turn.

Bowie was half-a-dozen lengths behind her, with power enough to catch up with her, but short on nerve. She had conned him into sneaking away from patrol for a few quick drinks at the club he frequented on leave. It was a crazy stunt to be pulling, but Dana was immune to his warnings. *What's the difference*, she had told him. *The High Command never listens to a word I have to say anyway, so why should I listen to them?*

Oh, he had argued with her, but as always she got the better of him.

"Hey, slow down!" he begged her from his cycle. "Are you crazy or something?"

It was a foolish question to be asking someone who had just walked out on patrol, so Bowie simply shook his head and gave the mecha more throttle.

The club (called Little Luna, an affectionate term for the Robotech Factory Satellite that had been in geo-synchronous orbit until the arrival of the alien ships) was SRO by the time Dana and Bowie arrived; it was body-to-body on the dance floor and tighter than that every-where else. But Bowie enjoyed a certain cachet because he played there so often, and it wasn't long before they had two seats at the bar.

"Let me have a bottle of your best Scotch," Dana told the bartender. She asked Bowie to join her, but he re-fused.

"I don't know what's bugging you," he said, "but don't you think you might be going about this the wrong way? I mean, getting thrown in the brig isn't going to prove any-thing—"

Dana silenced him by putting her hand over his mouth. Her attention was riveted on someone who had just ap-peared on-stage.

"Ladies and gentlemen, boys and girls, haves and have-nots," the deejay announced. "George Sullivan!"

Bowie moved Dana's hand aside and leaned around her. Sullivan was taking a quick bow for the crowd. He was a handsome man in his early thirties, on the old side for the following he enjoyed, and fairly conservative to boot. Clean shaven and wholesome looking, he wore his wavy brown hair in a kind of archaic pompadour, and liked to affect tailcoats with velvet lapels. Bowie could never understand his appeal, although he sang well enough.

"What a fox!" Dana commented.

Bowie made a face. "We jam together sometimes."

"You jam with that hunk? Bowie, I should have been coming to this club with you a long time ago."

Dana was too preoccupied to notice Bowie's shrug of indifference. "He's a newcomer." Sullivan had spotted Bowie and was leaving the stage and heading toward the bar, pawed at by some of the overeager. "He's coming over here," he told Dana quietly. "Don't make a driveling fool of yourself."

Dana's eyes lit up as Sullivan shook Bowie's hand. "I'm glad you stopped by, Bowie," Dana heard him say. "How would you feel about accompanying me on 'It's You'? I'm having some trouble with my romantic image."

Dana thought him even better-looking up close. And he smelled terrific. "That's hard to believe," she piped in.

Sullivan turned to her. "Have we met?" he said annoyed.

"This is Lieutenant Dana Sterling, George," said Bowie.

Sullivan stared at her: did his eyes narrow with interest just then, or did she imagine it, Dana asked herself? He was reaching for her hand. "A pleasure," she said, restraining herself from giving the masculine handshake she was accustomed to.

"*My* pleasure," said Sullivan, a bit too forcefully. He held on to her hand longer than he had to, communicating something with his eyes she could not fathom.

The three Masters stood before a towering curved wall of strobing lights and flashing schematics. Their hands reached out for the sensor pads of a control console.

"Vectors are coordinated," said number three. "Ready to override the Micronians' communications network."

"Let us begin immediately!" said Shaizan, aware too late of the haste implied by his tone. Bowkaz called him on it.

"Is this impatience? Now *you* are beginning to show signs of contamination!"

Shaizan growled slightly through clenched, vestigial teeth, yellow with age and disuse.

"Enough," said Dag, putting a quick end to the argument. "Commence override. . . ."

From his chambers in the United Earth Headquarters, Commander Leonard spoke with the Republic's prime minister via video-phone. A white-haired mustachioed politico who had served like Leonard under T. R. Edwards, Chairman Moran wore his badge of office on his right breast, and his sidearm to bed. He had learned tactics from Edwards, and that made him a dangerous man indeed.

"Your Excellency," Leonard said deferentially, "we must wait until we know more about the aliens before launching a preemptive strike. Frankly, my staff is split—"

"The final judgment is of course yours," the chairman interrupted. "But I hope you understand that it's becoming increasingly difficult for me to defend your inaction. If you're not up to it. . . ."

Leonard tried to keep his emotions in check as Moran left his threat unfinished. "I understand my obligations to the council," he said evenly.

Moran's head nodded in the monitor's field. "Good. I expect you to coordinate your attack plans as soon as possible."

The screen image de-rezzed and Leonard drew a hand down his face in frustration. *Curse Edwards for leaving me to this!* he said to himself.

But suddenly the screen was alive again: Leonard opened his eyes to wavering bars of static and multicolored contour lines. Then there was a voice attached to the oscillations—high-pitched and synthesized, though its message was clear.

"Consider this a final warning," it began. *"Interfere with our attempts to leave this planet and you face extinction."*

A second threat in as many minutes.

The monitor screen went blindingly white.

CHAPTER
NINE

Any assessment of T. R. Edwards's legacy must take into account the feudal structures his social and political programs fostered. It is not enough to say that the Council was organized along feudal lines; Human conventions and mores just as often reflect the nature of the ruling body as influence it. Feudalism ruled, both as political doctrine and spirit of the times, from the government on down to the constituency.

"Overlords," *History of the Second Robotech War,* Vol. CXII

DANA AND BOWIE SPENT TWO HOURS IN THE CLUB —two wonderful hours for Dana, talking with George, listening to him sing. He performed a medley of oldies, including several by Lynn-Minmei that were currently enjoying a revival. She sat at the piano, chin resting on her folded hands, while Bowie played and the audience applauded. And George sang for her. Afterwards he wanted to know all about her—Bowie, that dear, had often spoken of her to him—but he wanted to know more. All about her missions with the 15th, especially the recent one, when they had been responsible for bringing down the alien fortress. He let her go on and on—perhaps too far because of the Scotch she had consumed. But it had felt so good to get it all out, to talk to someone who was intensely interested in her life. In fact, he hardly talked about himself at all, and that was certainly something that set him apart from most of the men she met.

She was mounted on her Hovercycle now, waiting for

Bowie to say his good-byes and join her for the return trip to the barracks. Back to the real world. However, it was a different world than the one she looked out on only hours ago; fresh and revived, suddenly full of limitless possibilities.

Bowie appeared and swung one leg over his cycle.

"I can't get that last song out of my mind," Dana told him, stars in her eyes. "I've heard you mention George before, but why didn't you tell me he was so special?"

"Because I don't really know him that well," Bowie said. "He keeps to himself." He activated his cycle and strapped in while it warmed. "We better get a move on."

"Is he performing here again?" Dana wanted to know.

"Yeah, he's doing a set later tonight," Bowie returned absently. Then he noticed that Dana had switched off her cycle.

"Dana. . . ."

She was headed back into the club. "Don't worry about me. I just want to say good night. Take off. I'll catch up with you later."

Bowie sighed, exasperated, though he had little doubt she would catch up.

Dana went in through the stage entrance this time, noticing inside that some comedian had tampered with the sign above the door—instead of reading EXIT DOOR, it now read EXEDORE. The rear portion of the building was shared by an adjacent store, and there were numerous packing crates stacked here and there, and very little light. Dana called out to George in the darkness, and headed toward that meager light she could discern. Finally she heard the clacking of keyboard tabs and closed on that.

It was a small cubicle, brightly lit, with a cloth curtain for a doorway, and apparently served as both dressing room and office. George was seated at the desk, tapping data into a portable computer terminal. She called his name, but he was obviously too wrapped up in his task to hear her. So she waited silently by the door, wondering what he could be working on so diligently. Song lyrics, maybe, or a detailed account of the two hours they had just spent together. . . .

Dana looked again at the portable unit. There was something familiar about it. . . . Then she noticed the small insignia: the fluted column above the atomic circle . . . emblem of the *Global Military Police*!

Reflexively she drew in her breath and backed out of sight, hoping she hadn't tipped her hand. George had stopped. But then she heard him say: "Just as I thought . . . I suspected the enemy fortress had an outer hull weakness."

Pretty weird lyrics, thought Dana.

Cautiously, she peered into the room once again. Had she missed seeing someone, or was George talking to himself? Indeed, he was alone and a moment later gave voice to her worst fear:

"Now if I can just pry some more information out of the lovely Lieutenant Sterling, maybe I'll be able to put my theories to the test."

A detailed account of their two hours, all right, Dana said to herself. Sullivan was a GMP spy. And what those double-dealers couldn't pull from HQ, they hoped to learn from her! *And she had told them!* All about the raid on the fortress, the recon mission, the bio-gravitic network . . .

George muttered something, then surprised her further when she heard him say: "Oh, Marlene, if you were only here!"

She might have charged in at that moment if the stage manager hadn't appeared at the opposite door. "Five minutes," he told Sullivan.

Sullivan thanked the man and closed up the computer.

Dana backed away and ran to the exit door, her hand at her mouth.

* * *

The Masters were pleased with themselves, although each was now careful to avoid any displays that might be interpreted as emotional.

"Will they heed our warning?" Dag asked aloud.

"I can't believe they would be so foolish as to ignore it," said Bowkaz. He had been their voice to the Human commander.

Shaizan grunted. "All our questions will be answered soon enough."

"The time has come to signal the fleet."

Six hands reached forward to the console.

Dag removed his hands for an instant, breaking their link with the communicator. "Their behavior during the next few hours will indicate whether we have anything more to fear from them," he said darkly.

"Where have you been?" Angelo Dante said as Dana stormed into the 15th's barracks. The team was assembled in the rec room, talking tactics and stuffing their faces. Dana had heard warning Klaxons when she first entered the compound, but had no idea what they signaled.

"We've been looking all over for you, Lieutenant," from Sean now. "Where have you been?"

"Don't ask," Dana told them harshly. "Just tell me what's going on—are we slotted for patrol again?"

"Tomorrow morning," the sergeant explained. "Seems another enemy ship is on its way to Earth, probably to try and rendezvous with the grounded fortress. High command wants us there on the ground to meet 'em."

"They've already sent Marie up with a welcoming committee of TASC interceptors," Sean added. "Course they seem to forget we've got no way of fighting them until the bright boys down in data analysis give us some information."

Dana swallowed her initial surprise and smiled to herself.

"Sean, I've already taken care of that. I know where to get all the information we need."

They all froze, midaction, waiting for her to finish.

"That's right. I've got a way to get it straight from the GMP."

"What do they know that we don't know?" Louie asked her. "We're the ones who brought down that ship in the first place."

"But how do we know they didn't learn something from that Bioroid pilot?" Dana pointed out. "I find it awfully strange that he *expired*, just like that." She snapped her fingers. "They got something they're not telling us. Maybe they're even holding out on HQ. Why else would Fredericks have shown up at the zap tank? I'm telling you, the GMP is in on it."

"Even if you're right," Angelo said full of suspicion, "you and what army's gonna access that data?"

"Those files are top secret, eyes-only," Louie hastened to add.

"Come on," Dana laughed, throwing up her hands. "Give me a little credit, guys. One of their top agents is working for me—without his knowing it, of course."

It was enough to silence Angelo and tip the goggles off Louie's nose. Bowie and Sean just started at her.

The song came back to her as she took in their looks.

> *I always think of you*
> *Dream of you late at night*
> *What do you do*
> *When I turn out the light?*

You spy for the GMP, geek, Dana answered herself and the song. *But now it's you who's lost, George Sullivan. . . .*

The following morning (while Dana showered away

romantic feelings for George, decided that "Marlene" was probably some aging rock singer who wore too much makeup, and devised a plan to reverse the tables on suave Sullivan), Lieutenant Marie Crystal's TASC unit attacked the Earthbound fortress that had separated itself from the alien fleet to rendezvous with its grounded twin. Modified cargo shuttles had delivered the Black Lions to the edge of space and the assault was mounted with an absence of the usual preliminaries.

Leonard, Emerson, and the joint chiefs monitored the attack from the war room at Defense Headquarters.

"We're hitting them with everything we've got, but it's like water off a duck's back!" Leonard heard the lieutenant remark over the com net.

He would have been surprised to hear anything different; however, this was one time the chairman wasn't going to get the chance to accuse him of inaction. There was some hope early on that Crystal's squad could fell the fortress as Sterling's had the first, but apparently the aliens were quick to learn and not about to repeat mistakes: even if the Black Lions managed to disarm the defensive shields of the descending fortress, they would find the bio-gravitic reactor port sealed and unapproachable. And, as General Emerson had been quick to point out, having a second fortress crashland on Earth was not exactly optimum in any event. *Better to let them pick up their wreck,* Leonard said to himself as he studied the schematics on the situation board.

Leonard was trying hard not to think about the message that had been flashed across his monitor earlier that day, and had half convinced himself that it was an hallucination or the result of some plot hatched by Emerson's wing of the general staff meant to put him at further odds with Chairman Moran's Council.

"The assault group reports limited damage to the ship's superstructure," a controller reported now, "but the enemy's force shields remain intact and operational."

"The attack's having no effect whatsoever, Commander," Emerson said angrily.

Leonard adopted the same tone. "Then we'll destroy the grounded ship before this one can arrive to save it."

Emerson grinned wryly. *Just who was the commander kidding?* Perhaps he was uttering these absurdities for posterity, Rolf thought. *Leonard had the right idea,* they would say. *Leonard did everything he could.* Save for the fact everyone knew that the destruction of either fortress wasn't within their power. Nevertheless, the Tactical Armored units would be deployed to realize Leonard's grandiose lies.

Or at least die trying.

Dana had asked Bowie to find out where George lived. Her friend found it hard to believe that she could think about love at a time like this (*lust* was the term he actually used), but he relented and came through. She regretted having to keep him in the dark about her plan; however, she didn't want him going into battle with any more on his mind than was absolutely necessary.

Once again she put Dante in temporary command of the unit and set out on her private mission, trailing Sullivan from his low-rent apartment not far from the GMP ministry, to a grassy overlook in a restricted area on the outskirts of the city. It was a tedious challenge, since George had opted to hike to the spot. But once Dana was sure of his destination, she powered her Hovertank along the back roads that led to the overlook and arrived shortly after he did.

He was standing under perhaps the only shade tree on the entire ridgeline, his computer briefcase clutched in his left hand. "What in the world are you doing way out here?" he said, when she called to him from the mecha's cockpit. "Shouldn't you be with your squadron or something?"

"I couldn't bear to be away from you any longer," she

told him dramatically. "And I was hoping I could get you to join my team . . . unless you have to report back to the GMP?"

George stepped back from the mecha as though he had been hit. Dana dismounted and told him not to worry about it—his secret was safe with her.

"But you used me," she said, unconcealed hurt in her voice. "And I want to know why. What are you trying to prove?"

Sullivan's face registered anger. "I'm not trying to prove anything." Then he closed his eyes for a moment and shook his head. "All right," he said after a moment. "But I've never told this to anyone."

Dana kept quiet while he explained. His sister had been a casualty of the first alien raid on Monument City, and Sullivan, then an HQ war department tech, blamed himself for her death—he had forgotten to pick her up after school and she had been caught up in the attack while waiting for him.

The sort of story Dana had heard all too frequently and become somewhat inured to, despite the sympathy she felt for him. One might as well blame chance or fate, she told herself as Sullivan continued.

He had deserted his post to visit her in the hospital and—though severely burned and not expected to last the night—she had spoken his name as if nothing had happened, assigning no blame and concerned that he would soon be alone in the world. That was when the military police had arrived on the scene; they had come to arrest him, but when they understood the depth of his grief they realized that he was someone they could use for their own purposes. He had been with them ever since, playing both sides of the fence whenever he could.

"So you've been waging a one-man campaign against your sister's murderers," Dana said when he finished.

"Whenever I can," he told her.

"Tell me one thing: does the GMP have new information about the fortress—vulnerable spots or weaknesses, some place we could hit them and incapacitate them?"

George nodded gravely, aware that he was breaking his security oath. "Yes. We have reason to believe that we do."

"And it's in that computer of yours?"

Again he nodded.

Dana smiled and took hold of his hand. "Well then, let's put what you've learned to good use." She led him back to the Hovertank and gestured to the rumble seat. "With your data and my firepower, we can send these alien invaders packing."

With annihilation discs raining down on them from all sides, the 15th was throwing everything they had against the enemy, often successfully when it came to downing trios of Hoversled Bioroids (especially in Dana's absence), but ineffectually in terms of their primary target —the fortress itself. Reports from Headquarters indicated that Crystal's Black Lion team had fared no better with the incoming ship, now visible in the explosion-filled sky above the angry ridgeline.

"These guys are slippery little devils!" Sean said over the net. "What does it take to nail them?"

"Keep your eyes open and I'll show you," Dante radioed back.

They both had their mecha in Gladiator mode, their cannons disgorging ear-splitting volleys without letup.

Dante ranged in his weapon and blew one of the airborne Bioroids to debris, just after it loosed a shot that managed to topple Sean's tank.

"Everything okay?" Dante asked when Sean righted the thing.

"I'll live, if that's what you mean."

"I was talkin' about the tank," the sergeant told him.

This from a guy he had once out-ranked, Sean muttered to himself. "Thanks for your concern, Sarge."

Then all at once Dana's *Valkyrie* was in their midst, oddly enough with a civilian passenger in the rumble seat. Bowie identified the stranger for the team and the tac net was nothing but nasty comments for a minute or so. Sean got in the last word: "Hey Lieutenant, I didn't know you went for thrill-freaks!"

"Just cut the chatter and give me some cover," Dana ordered.

Full-out, her tank was making directly for the fortress, unswerving in the face of the ground fire it was receiving from Bioroid troops holding the perimeter. Sean watched her go airborne as the tank crested a small rise less than one-hundred yards from the ship, then lost her in the blinding flashes of plasma light Alphas and Falcons were pouring against the fortress's defensive shield.

A trio of Hovercrafts pursued Dana as she skimmed the tank across the ship's armored surface, annihilation discs winging past George's unprotected head as he studied the computer readouts. Had her helmet not been essential for rapport with the mecha, Dana would have handed it back to him.

"Have you coordinated the data yet?"

"It keeps shifting," he yelled into the wind.

"Keep trying," she urged him, piloting the tank through four lanes of disc fire.

They had already made one pass over the fortress and she now veered the tank around for a second, taking out a hovercraft as she completed the break. There was no time to place her shots and she was sorry for that; but if Sullivan's computer did its job, the end would more than justify the means. Relying on the mecha's lateral guns, her hands locked on the handlebar-like control and trigger mechanisms, she thumbed a second and third Bioroid to destruction.

Meanwhile the second fortress was eclipsing the sky overhead, threatening to sandwich her small craft between it and the grounded ship. Tactical units were loosing cannon rounds against its plated underbelly, only adding to her predicament as the shells often ricocheted and detonated along the Hovertank's course. Dana had also noticed Logans overhead before the fortress blocked her view; possibly the remnants of Marie Crystal's Black Lion squadron.

"The vulnerable area will be exposed when the fortresses attempt a ship-to-ship link up," Sullivan said at last. "That'll be the time to hit them!"

Dana looked up, trying to calculate how much time they had left before the fortress rendered her and her new sweetie a memory. The ventral surface of the ship was an ugly sight, like the mouth of some techno-spider about to devour them.

"I'm patching the information directly into your onboard computers, Dana. The rest is up to you."

"Leave it to me," she started to say, accelerating the mecha through the narrowing gap formed by the two ships. But suddenly a Hovercraft had appeared out of nowhere, raining rear energy hyphens at her. Then a Bioroid swooped in from her port side, forcing her dangerously close to some sort of radar glove, a small mountain on the hull of the ship. As she swerved to avoid it, she lost George.

She heard his scream as he flew out of the rumble seat, and craned her head around just in time to see him caught in the metalshod fist of a Hovercraft pilot.

Dana swung around hard, but lost sight of the alien craft. But Marie Crystal was on the net telling her that she had seen the near collision and had the enemy right in front of her.

Dana couldn't figure out what Marie was doing in the gap, but she didn't stop to think about it. She shot forward and attained the open skies again, scanning for Marie's Logan-mode Veritech.

Below her, one of her teammates had just reconfigured from tank to Guardian mode and loosed a bolt at one of the alien sky-sleds. Dana had a sinking feeling as she traced the shot's trajectory: it caught the Bioroid that was holding George, sending it careening into a fiery spin, and on a collision course with Marie's fighter.

Crystal broke too late, impacting against the out-of-control sled and falling into a spin of her own. Dana didn't know who to watch: the Bioroid holding Sullivan or Marie. Suddenly the tank that had fired off that fateful round—Sean's tank—was reconfiguring to Battloid, and leaping up to *catch* Crystal's ship. Despite her fascination, Dana involuntarily averted her eyes; but when she looked again, both Veritechs were reasonably intact.

Then all at once there was an explosion at nine o'clock. She turned, as her mecha was rocked by the shockwaves.

The Bioroid was history.

And George Sullivan was dead.

She screamed his name and flew into the face of the angry fireball, hoping, expecting to find who knew what. And as her scorched tank emerged she recalled his last words to her: *The rest is up to you.*

Inside the grounded fortress, the Masters watched a schematic display of their descending rescuer, a hundred yards overhead now and already extending the grapplers and tendrils that would secure the link-up.

"We are ready," Dag reported.

Shaizan nodded eagerly. "Good. Deploy the Zor clone toward their strongest defenses. . . . We must make certain that he is conveniently captured by the Micronians. . . ."

One minute Angelo Dante was sitting in the cockpit of the Gladiator doing his lethal best, and the next thing he knew he was airborne, turning over and over. . . .

He hit the ground with a thud that knocked the breath from his lungs and left him unconscious for a moment. When the world refocused itself, he recognized what was left of his mangled Hovertank, toppled on its side and burning.

Dante got to his feet, promising to tear the aliens apart, even as a sledded Bioroid dropped in for the kill. It was that gleaming red job, Angelo noticed, already outside himself and braving it out, the hero he was born to be. But just then a strange thing happened: a pinpoint blast from the fortress bull's-eyed the Hovercraft, sending sled and pilot into a fiery crash in the craggy outcroppings near the Earth Forces front lines.

Dante heard an atonal scream of agony issue from the craft as it fell.

"They shot down their own guy!" a puzzled Dante said out loud, figuring he would live to see another day after all. . . .

Dana tried to erase the fiery image of Sullivan's death as she piloted the Hovertank back toward the fortress once again. Split-screen data schematics were running parallel across the monitor screen of *Valkyrie*'s targeting computer, directing the mecha's weapons systems to the coordinates that would spell doom for the fortress. And by the look of things, there wasn't much time left.

With the rescue ship overhead now, the grounded fortress was actually lifting off, still the target of countless warheads that were exploding harmlessly against the alloyed hull—its complex network of close-in weaponry silent—and apparently drawing on all the reserve power available to it. The entire ridgeline appeared to be effected by its leave-taking; a deafening roar filled the air, and the ground was rumbling, sending rock and shale sliding down the steep slopes of those unnatural tors. Massive whirlwinds of gravel and debris spun from the underside of the ascending ship, as though loosed from traps set an eternity ago.

As Dana closed on the twin fortresses, she could see that four panels had opened along the dorsal side of the first, revealing massive socketlike connectors, sized to accept shafts—glowing like outsize radio tubes—that were telescoping from circular portals in the bulbous, spiny anchor shown by the second.

"Faster!" Dana urged her Hovertank, the cockpit screen flashing, the parallel series of schematics aligned. Then the mecha was suddenly reconfiguring to Gladiator mode, retroing to an abrupt halt, the cannon already traversing and ranging in. Having surrendered to the dictates of the computer, Dana could do nothing but sit back and pray that she had arrived in time.

The fortresses were linked in an obscene technomating, one atop the other, ascending and accelerating now, scarcely a three-meter wide gap between them.

Dana's mecha fired once, its energy bolt finding that narrow interface and detonating squarely against the linkup anchor. On all sides, explosive light erupted from the empty space between the ships, and the upper fortress seemed to shudder, list, and collapse over its mate.

But the ships continued to rise.

"It can't be!" Dana shouted over the net. "Why didn't it work?!" Even as she said it, though, she knew the answer. The computer was flashing its internal debriefing to her, but she didn't need to double-check the screen for what she knew in her guts: she had been a split-second too late, two-hundred yards out of the required lethal cone.

Dana had one last look at the fortresses before they disappeared into battle clouds and smoke, a close encounter of the worst kind.

CHAPTER
TEN

I think I sensed something about the alien pilot even before Cochran turned to me with the results of his findings. Even now I can't say where that feeling originated or where my present thoughts are directed. I only know that the moment seemed full of import and grand purpose; something about the alien triggered a change in me that is beginning to overshadow my entire life.

From the personal journal of Major General Rolf Emerson

GENERAL EMERSON'S OFFICIAL CAR (A BLACK Hoverlimo with large tail fins, a purely decorative vintage front grill, and an antique, winged hood ornament) tore from the Ministry's parking lot at a little after three o'clock on the morning following the liftoff of the enemy fortresses. Rolf was in the backseat, silent and contemplative, while his young aide, Lieutenant Milton, felt compelled to issue cautions. Monument City felt like a ghost town.

Emerson had logged two hours of sleep when the call from Alan Fredericks of the **GMP had** awakened him: something interesting had been **discovered** near the liftoff site—an alien pilot, alive and apparently well.

Rolf asked himself what Fredericks was up to: he had brought the alien to Miles Cochran's lab, and had yet to inform Commander Leonard of his find. With rivalry running high between the GMP and the militaristic faction of the general staff, Fredericks's position was suspect. Perhaps, however, this was merely the GMP's way of making up for the hatchet job they did on the first captured Bioroid pilot. Emerson knew when he recradled the handset exactly what he could be setting himself up for but felt the risk justified. He had asked Colonel Rochelle to rendezvous with him at Cochran's lab, then called for his car.

"This is going to look suspicious, sir," Milton told him for the third time. "The chief of staff racing out of the Ministry in the middle of the night without telling anyone where he's going."

"I know what I'm doing, *Captain*," Rolf said brusquely, hoping to put an end to the man's ceaseless badgering.

"Yes, sir," the lieutenant replied, sullenly.

Emerson had already turned away from him to stare out the window once again. *At least* I hope *I know what I'm doing*, he thought. . . .

Rochelle, Fredericks, and Nova Satori were already waiting at Cochran's high-tech lab on the outskirts of Monument City. The good doctor himself, a bit of a privateer who walked that no-man's land between the GMP and the general staff, was busy keeping the Bioroid pilot alive.

Emerson stared down at the alien now from the observation balcony above one of the lab's IC rooms. Cochran had the handsome elfin-featured young android on its back, an IV drip running, a trach insert in its neck. The pilot was apparently naked under the bedsheets, and surrounded by banks of monitoring and scanning apparatus.

"Our last captive died through *official* mishandling," Rolf was telling the others, his back turned to them. "I want to make certain that doesn't happen again."

"Yes, sir," Fredericks spoke for the group.

Rolf swung around to face the three of them. "Who found him?"

Nova Satori, the GMP's attractive raven-haired lieutenant, stepped forward and offered salute. "I did, sir. Out where the fortress was."

Emerson's eyebrows beetled. "What were you doing out there, Lieutenant?"

Satori and Fredericks exchanged nervous looks. "Uh, she was looking for one of our agents," Fredericks said.

Emerson looked hard at the hawk-faced colonel. "And just what was one of your agents doing out there?"

Fredericks cleared his throat. "We're trying to determine that ourselves, General."

Satori related her brief explanation, purposely keeping George Sullivan's name out of it. But it was the singer/spy she had been looking for; more important, the terminal he'd been carrying when last seen—something Dana Sterling had better be able to account for. Nova had heard sounds coming from one of the downed Hovercrafts and upon investigation had discovered the alien pilot. He was ambulatory then, but collapsed soon after being taken into custody, as though someone had suddenly shifted him to standby mode.

"And he seems fluent in English," Nova concluded.

"All the more reason to let Cochran handle this personally," said Emerson. "And as of this moment I want an absolute information blackout regarding the prisoner."

Rochelle was saying little, waiting for Emerson to finish; but he now felt compelled to address the issue that had been plaguing him since the general's phonecall some hours before. It was a privilege of sorts to be included in Emerson's clique, but not if it was going to mean a court-martial.

"General," he said at last, "are you proposing that we keep this from Commander Leonard?"

Satori and Fredericks were hanging on Emerson's reply.

"I am," he told them evenly.

"Exactly *what* do you want us to do with the specimen?" Fredericks asked after a moment.

"I want you to run every test you can think of on him. I need to know how these creatures breathe, think, eat— do you understand me? And I need the information *yesterday*."

"Yessir," the three said in unison.

Just then Professor Cochran stepped into the observation room, removing his surgical mask and gloves, while everyone questioned him. He waited for the voices to die down and looked into each face before speaking, a slightly bemused expression on his face.

"I have one important fact to report straightaway." He turned and gestured down to the Bioroid pilot. "This *alien* . . . is Human."

The three Masters summoned their Scientist triumvirate to the command center of the newly ascended fortress. The Zor clone had survived and was presently in the hands of the Micronians. The functioning neurosensor that had been implanted in the clone's brain told them this much, although there were as yet no visuals. Schematics that filled the chamber's oval screen showed that some damage had been sustained, but all indications suggested it was nothing that need concern them. It was clear, however, that the Scientists did not share their Masters' enthusiasm for the plan.

"By capturing the Zor clone, the Micronians have played right into our hands," Shaizan said by way of defense. It was certainly unnecessary that he *explain* himself to the triumvirate, but it was clear that a certain rebelliousness was in the air, pervasive throughout the ship, and Shaizan hoped to lay some of that to rest. "They themselves will lead us to the Protoculture Matrix."

"And suppose the Micronians should attack us again?" the lavender-haired androgyne asked defiantly.

"One purpose of the neuro-sensor is to keep us appraised of all their military activities," Bowkaz told him, indicating the screen schematics. "We will have ample warning."

"Yes...and what happens if the Micronians should discover your *precious* neuro-sensor? What then?"

"Discover it?" Shaizan raised his voice. "That's absurd! Recording of the hyper-frequency of the device is far beyond the realm of their crude scientific instruments. The idea is ludicrous!"

The scientist scowled. "Let us hope so," his synthesized voice seemingly hissed.

Dana felt Sean's gentle tap on her shoulder and heard a forearm chord of sharps and flats. She opened her eyes to sunrise, distant crags like arthritic fingers reaching up into pink and grey layers of sky. She had fallen asleep at the ready-room's piano, although it took her a moment to realize this, head pillowed on forearms folded across the keyboard. Sean was standing behind her, apologizing for disturbing her, making some joke about her guarding the eighty-eights all night and asking if she wanted some breakfast. The rest of the 15th were scattered about the room, arguing and moping about by the looks of it.

"...And who the hell was snoring all night?" she heard Angelo ask in his loudest voice. "Somebody sounded like a turbo-belt earth-mover with a faulty muffler."

Louie was off in a corner tinkering with some gadget that looked like a miniature Bioroid. Bowie was sullenfaced in another, distanced from the scene by earphones.

"I couldn't sleep a wink," Dana told Sean weakly. She remembered now that she had been thinking of Sullivan and his senseless death, been trying to peck out the melody of that old Lynn-Minmei tune. . . .

"You need to cut loose of that responsibility once in a while," the former lieutenant was telling her. "Let your hair down and have some fun, take life a little less seriously."

Dana got up, reached for the glass of juice she had left on top of the piano, and went to refill it at the dispenser. "There's a war going on, pal," she said, pushing past Sean. "Course you're not the first soldier I've run across who's found the call of the wild more attractive than the call of duty."

"Look who's talking," Sean laughed.

"I mean, I wouldn't want to think that the war was interfering with anything, *Private.*"

"I don't let it cramp my style, *Dana.*"

Style? she thought, sipping at the juice. *Let me count the comebacks to that one.* . . . But as she said this to herself, fragments of last night's dream began to surface. There was George, of course, but then he became all mixed up with the images of that long-haired Bioroid pilot she and Bowie had crossed lasers with weeks ago—*Zor!* And then somehow her mother had appeared in the dream, telling her things she couldn't summon up now. . . .

". . . and I'm definitely not into hopeless romances."

Dana whirled, not sure whether she should be angry, having missed his intro; but she saw that Sean was gesturing to Bowie.

"Now here's a guy who was operating just fine up until a few weeks ago. Now he's out there where the shuttles don't run. And for a *dream*-girl at that!"

Bowie didn't hear a word of this, which Dana figured was just as well. Sean made a few more lame comments as he left the room. Dana went over to her friend and positioned herself where she could be seen, if not heard.

"Sean says you're upset," Dana said when he removed the headphones.

Bowie made a face. "What does he know?"

"It's that alien dame," said Sergeant Dante from across the room, his nose buried in the newspaper. "You better set your sights on something a little more down to earth, my friend."

Dana threw Angelo a look he could feel clear through

the morning edition. "Just like that, huh Sergeant? He just snaps his fingers and forgets her."

"For cryin' out loud, she's an *alien*! . . . Uh, no offense, of course," he hastened to add.

"No offense taken," Dana told him. "I know your type can't help it. But I don't care if this girl Musica is 'Spider-woman,' Angelo. You can't tell someone to just turn her heart on and off like a light switch."

"*Her* heart, Dana? *Her* heart?"

Dana had her mouth opened to say something, but she noticed that Bowie was crying. When she put her hand on his shoulder, he shrugged it off roughly, stood up, and ran from the room.

Dana started to chase him, but thought better of it halfway down the corridor. *Did her father have to put up with this from his squad?* she wondered. *Did her mother? And where were they,* she asked the ceiling—*where?!*

Lieutenant Marie Crystal had slept well enough, thanks to the anodynes she received at the base hospital after the crash of her ship. But the pills' effects had worn off now, and she couldn't locate a joint or muscle in her body that wasn't crying out for more of the same medication. She reached out for the bedside hand mirror and took a glance at her disheveled, pale reflection. Fortunately her face didn't look as bad as the rest of her felt. It was deathly hot and dry in the room, so she cautiously got out of bed, shaking as she stood, and changed out of the hospital gown into a blue satin robe someone had been thoughtful enough to drop by the room. She left it open as she climbed back under the sheets; after all, it wasn't as if she were expecting visitors or anything.

But no sooner had that thought crossed her mind when she heard Sean's voice outside the door. Having literally landed in the arms of the Southern Cross's ace womanizer was perhaps only a shade better than having piled into a mountain, but it was something she was going to have to live with for a while. She hadn't, however, anticipated that the trials were to begin so soon.

Marie ran a hand through her short, unruly hair and pulled the robe closed; Sean was running into some Nightingale flack at the door.

"Couldn't I just have five minutes with her?" Marie heard Sean say. "Just to drop off these pretty flowers that I picked with my own teeth?"

The nurse was resolute: no one was permitted to enter.

"But I'm the guy who practically saved her life! Listen: I won't talk to her or make her laugh or cry or anything —really—"

"No visitors means no visitors," the nurse told him.

Just whose side is she on? Marie began to wonder.

"Well isn't it just my luck to find the one nurse in this whole hospital who's immune to my many charms."

Now *that* sounded like the Sean Marie knew.

"Here," she heard him say now. "You keep the flowers. Who knows, maybe we'll just meet again, dar-lin'."

Marie's pale blue eyes went wide.

She was wrong: landing in the arms of his Battloid was *worse* than having crashed!

General Emerson was in the war room when Leonard finally caught up with him. He had been dodging the commander's messages all day, victimized by a dark pre-monition that Leonard had somehow learned about the alien pilot. And as soon as Leonard opened his mouth, Emerson knew that his instincts had been correct. But strangely enough, the commander seemed to be taking the whole thing in stride.

"I've been told that you're keeping a secret from me, General Emerson," Leonard began, with almost a lilt to his voice. "I thought I'd come over here and ask you my-self: is it true that another Bioroid specimen had been captured?"

"Yes, Commander," Rolf returned after saluting. "As a matter of fact, Professor Cochran is running a complete series of tests on him."

Leonard suddenly whirled on him red-faced with anger.

"Just when were you planning to tell me about *him*, General?!"

Techs throughout the room swiveled from their duty stations.

"Or perhaps you were considering *keeping* this information from me!" Leonard was bellowing.

Rolf didn't even get the chance to stammer his half-formed explanation.

"I'm taking the prisoner out of your hands, General. He'll be analyzed by military scientists, not renegade professors, do you understand me?"

Rolf fought to keep down his own anger while Leonard stormed off, his boot heels loud against the acrylic floor in the otherwise silent room. "We mustn't let this prisoner be destroyed," he managed to get out without yelling. "We learned *nothing* from the last one. This time we must proceed impartially, and Miles Cochran's our best hope for that."

The commander had stopped in his tracks and swung around to face Emerson, regarding him head to toe before responding. And when he spoke his voice was loud but controlled.

"I'm sure our people could do just as well, General. But it seems to me that you've taken a personal interest in this prisoner. Am I correct?"

"I have," said Emerson, and Leonard nodded knowingly.

"Is there something more I should know about this particular *android*?"

Rolf was tight-lipped. "Not at the moment, Commander."

"Well then, since you're so . . . *determined*. . . . But

keep in mind that this one is *your* responsibility, General. There are too many variables in this situation already."

Emerson saluted and Leonard was turning to leave, when all at once a novel blip appeared on the threat board. The power play forgotten, all eyes focused on the screen. Every terminal in the room was clacking out paper. Techs were hunched over their consoles, trying to make sense of the thing that had just appeared in sub-lunar orbit *out of nowhere*!

"What is it?" demanded Leonard, his hands pressed to the command console. "Someone answer me!"

"A ship, sir," said a female enlisted-rating. "And it appears to be moving in to engage the enemy!"

CHAPTER
ELEVEN

Major Carpenter and crew left today. "Lang's shot in the dark," as some are calling it. But I have already let it be known that the responsibility is mine, and one part of me is even envious of their leavetaking. Simply to attempt a return to Earth, to quit this malignant corner of space, this crazed and maniacal warfare against our own brothers and sisters and the unstopable creatures borne of the Tirolians' savagery and injustice. . . . It is clear to me that my destiny lies elsewhere, perhaps on Optera itself, Lisa my life and strength beside me.

The Collected Journals of Admiral Rick Hunter

THE SHIP THAT HAD MATERIALIZED FROM HYPERspace and created that blip on the threat board was long overdue in arriving in Earthspace. Ten years was hardly a measurable quantity by galactic standards; but to a planet brought once to the brink of extinction and now enmeshed in a war that threatened what little remained, ten years was an eternity—and the appearance of the ship a godsend. Unfortunately such feelings were soon to prove premature. . . .

Lost in space for the past five Earth-years—lost in corridors of time, in continuum shifts and as yet unmapped mobius loops—the cruiser had finally found its way home. Before that, it had been part of the Pioneer Expeditionary Mission—that ill-fated attempt to reach the homeworld of the Robotech Masters before the Masters' sinister hands reached out for Earth. The Mission, and that wondrous ship constructed in space and launched from Little Luna, had had such noble beginnings. The Protoculture Matrix thought to have been hidden inside the SDF-1 by its alien creator, Zor, had never been located; the war between Earth and the Zentraedi terminated. So what better step to take, but a diplomatic one: an effort to erase all possibilities of a second war by coming to terms with peace beforehand.

But how could the members of the SDF-3 have known —the Hunters, Lang, Breetai, Exedore and the rest— how could they have foreseen what awaited them on Tirol and what treacherous part T. R. Edwards would come to play in the unfolding of events? Earth itself would have no knowledge of these things for years to come: of the importance of a certain element indigenous to the giant planet Fantoma, of a certain quasi-canine creature native to Optera, of a budding young genius named Louie Nichols. . . .

For the moment, therefore, the cruiser being tracked by Earth Defcon seemed like the answer to a prayer.

The ship was a curious, one-of-a-kind hybrid, fabricated on the far side of the galactic core by the Robotechnicians of the SDF-3 before the schism between Hunter and Edwards, for the express purpose of hyperspace experimentation: the SDF-3 hadn't the means to return to Earth, but it was conceivable that a small ship could accomplish what its massive parent could not. Those conversant with Robotech warship classifications could point to the Zentraedi influences on this one, notably the cruiser's sleek sharklike form, and the elevated bridge and astrogation centers that rose like a dorsal fin just aft of its blunted bow. But if its hull was alien, its Reflex power center was pure Terran, especially the quadripartite design of the triple-thruster units that comprised the stern.

The cruiser's commander, Major John Carpenter, had distinguished himself during the Tirolian campaign against the Invid, but five-years in hyperspace (was it five minutes or five lifetimes, who could say which?) had taken their toll. Not only on Carpenter, but on the entire crew, every one of them a victim of a space sickness that had no name except madness, perhaps.

When the ship had emerged from hyperspace and a vision of their blue-and-white homeworld had filled the forward viewports, there wasn't a crewman aboard who believed his eyes. They had all experienced the cruel tricks that awaited the unwary techno-voyager, the *horrors*.... Then they had identified the massive spade fortresses of the alien fleet. And there was no mistaking these, no mistaking the intent of the soulless Masters who guided them.

Carpenter had ordered an immediate attack, convinced that Admiral Hunter himself would have done the same. And if it seemed *insane*, the commander told himself as Veritech teams tore from the cruiser's ports—one relatively undersized ship against so many—one had merely to recall what the SDF-1 had done against *four million*!

Even the strategy was to be the same: all firepower would be concentrated against the flagship of the alien fleet; that destroyed, the rest would follow.

But Carpenter's crew put too much stock in history, which, despite claims to the contrary, rarely repeats itself. More important, Carpenter forgot exactly *who* he was dealing with: after all, these weren't the Zentraedi... these were *the beings who had created the Zentraedi*!

In the command center of the alien flagship the three Masters exchanged astonished looks over the rounded crown of the Protoculture cap. Lifting their eyes to the bridge readout screens, the look the three registered could almost have passed for amusement: a warship even more primitive in design than those the Earth Forces had sent against them in the recent past had just de-folded from hyperspace and was attempting to engage the fleet singlehandedly.

"Absurd," Bowkaz commented.

"Perhaps we should add *insult* to the list of strategies they have attempted to use against us."

"Primitive and barbaric," said Dag, observing how the fortress's segmented cannons were annihilating the Earth mecha, as though they were a swarm of mites. "We do them a service by obliterating them. They insult themselves with such gestures."

Behind the Masters the Scientist triumvirate was grouped at its duty station.

"We have locked on their battle cruiser at mark six bearing five-point-nine," one of them reported now.

Shaizan regarded the screen. "Prepare for a change in plans," he told the blue-haired clone. "Ignore the drones and deal directly with the cruiser. All units will converge on your coordinates. Our ship will hold the lead . . . for the glory of the kill."

The techs, staff, and officers in the war room were still yahooing and celebrating the return of the Pioneer Mission. Supreme Commander Leonard had left immediately to confer with Chairman Moran, leaving General Emerson in charge of the surprise situation.

"Sir!" said one of the techs. "Pioneer Commander is requesting backup. Shall we scramble our fighters and Ghosts?"

Emerson grunted his assent and nodded, curiously uneasy, almost alarmed by the sudden turn of events. Was it possible, he asked as the techs sounded the call—the return of his old friends, a new beginning? . . .

Bowie and Dana, each cocooned in private thoughts, sequels to earlier interrupted musings, were in the 15th's rec room when they heard the scramble alert.

"All pilots to battle stations, all pilots to battle stations. . . . All ground crews to staging areas six through sixteen. . . . Prepare fighters for rendezvous with SDF-3 attack wing!"

Dana was on her feet even before the final part of the call, disregarding as always the particulars and details. Rushing past Bowie, she grabbed his arm and practically hauled him into the barracks corridor, where everyone was double-timing it toward the drop-racks and mecha ports. She hadn't seen such frenzy, such *enthusiasm*, in months, and wondered about the cause. Either the city was under full-scale attack or something miraculous had happened.

She saw Louie racing by and called for him to stop. "Hey, what's all the ruckus about?!" she asked him, Bowie breathless by her side.

Louie returned a wide grin, eyes bright even through the ever-present goggles. "It seems the cavalry's arrived in the nick of time! We've got reinforcements from hyperspace—the Pioneer's come home!"

Dana and Bowie almost fell over.

Something miraculous had *happened!*

"We need a miracle, John," Commander Carpenter's navigator said hopelessly. "We've thrown everything but the kitchen sink at them. Nothing's penetrating those shields."

The two men were on the bridge of the cruiser, along with a dozen other officers and techs who had wordlessly witnessed the utter destruction of their strike force. *That those men who had lived through so much terror should perish at Earth's front gate,* Carpenter thought, half out of his mind from the horror of it. But he was determined that their deaths count for *something*.

"Have the first wing make an adjustment to fifty-seven mark four-nine," he started to say when the cruiser sustained its first blow.

Carpenter was sent reeling across the bridge by the force of the impact, and several techs were knocked from their chairs. He didn't have to be told how serious it was but asked for damage reports nevertheless.

"Our shields are down," the navigator updated. "Ruptured. Primary starboard thrusters have all been neutralized."

"Enemy fortress right behind us, Commander!" said a second.

In shock, Carpenter glanced at the screens. "Divert all auxiliary power to the port thrusters! All weapons astern —*fire at will!*"

"What the devil's going on up there?!" Leonard shouted as he paced in front of the war room's Big Board.

Rolf Emerson turned from one of the balcony consoles to answer him. "We've lost all communication with them, Commander."

Leonard made a motion of disgust. "What about our support wing?"

"The same," Emerson said evenly.

Leonard whirled on the situation screen, raised and waved his fist, a gesture as meaningful as it was pathetic.

A radiant rash broke out across the pointed bow of the Masters' flagship, pinpoints of blinding energy that burst a nanosecond later, emitting devastating lines of hot current that ripped into the helpless cruiser, destroying in a series of explosions the entire rear quarter of the ship.

More than half the bridge crew lay dead or dying now; Carpenter and his second were torn up and bloodied but alive. The cruiser, however, was finished, and the major knew it.

"Ready all escape pods," he ordered, the heel of his hand to a severe head wound. "Evacuate the crew."

The navigator carried out the command, initiating the ship's self-destruct sequence as he did so.

"We're locked on a collision course with one of the fortresses," he told his commander. "Seventeen seconds to impact." Throwing a final switch, he added: "I'm sorry, sir."

"Don't apologize," Carpenter said, meeting his gaze. "We did what we could."

On a lifeless plateau above Monument City, Dana and Sean, side-by-side in the cramped forward seats of a Hovertransport, watched the skies. The rest of the 15th were not far off. Escape pods from the defeated Pioneer ship were drifting down almost lazily out of azure skies, gleaming metallic spheres hung from brightly colored chutes. Taking in this tranquil scene, one would have been hard pressed to imagine the one they had inhabited only moments before, the heavenly inferno from which they had been dropped.

Dana had learned the sad truth: it had not been the SDF-3 out there, but a single ship long separated from its parent. Like herself. The crew's last-ditch effort to hurtle the cruiser into one of the six alien fortresses had proved futile. Still, she had hopes that one among the valiant survivors who were now stepping burned and damaged from the escape pods would have some words for her personally, some message, even one five or fifteen years old.

Sean maneuvered their Hovertruck toward one of the pods that had landed in their area. Dana leapt out and approached the sphere, welcoming home its two bloodied passengers, and doing what little she could to dress their facial wounds. The men were roughly the same height, pale and atrophied-looking after their many years in space and badly shaken from their recent ordeal. The older of the two, who had brown hair, a wide-eyed albeit handsome face, introduced himself as Major John Carpenter.

Dana told them her name and held her breath.

Carpenter and the other officer looked at one another.

"Max Sterling's daughter?" Carpenter said, and Dana felt her knees grow weak.

"Do you know my parents?!" she asked eagerly. "Tell me . . . are they . . . ?"

Carpenter put his hand on her shoulder. "They were when we last saw them, Lieutenant. But that was five years ago."

Dana exhaled loudly. "You've got to tell me everything."

Carpenter smiled weakly and was about to say something more when his companion grasped him by the upper arm meaningfully. Again the two looked at each other, exchanging some unvoiced signal.

"Lieutenant," the major said after a moment. "I'm afraid that will have to wait until I speak with Commander Leonard."

"But—"

"That means now, Lieutenant Sterling," Carpenter said more firmly.

Supreme Commander Leonard hadn't logged many hours in deep space, but he was familiar enough with the ups and downs to recognize a case of vacuum psychosis when he saw it; and that's exactly what he felt he and General Emerson were up against while listening to the mad ravings of Major Carpenter and his equally space-happy navigator. In Leonard's office at the Ministry, the two men rambled on about the Pioneer Expeditionary Mission, repeatedly referring to a schism among the Earth Forces—T. R. Edwards on the one side, Admiral Hunter and some group calling itself the *Sentinels* on the other. But in spite of it all, High Command's principal question had been answered: these aliens were indeed the Robotech Masters. They had abandoned their homeworld of Tirol and traveled across the galaxy to Earthspace; and it was beginning to seem obvious to Leonard that they had not come to *reclaim* anything, but to destroy the Human race and lay claim to and colonize the planet itself.

The two injured officers had concerns of their own, as anyone would after fifteen long years offworld, and the commander did his best to answer these without breaching security. He described the initial appearance of the Robotech ships; the fighting centered around the lunar base and space station *Liberty*; the voluntary disappearance of the Robotech Factory Satellite by the Zentraedi who operated it.

Leonard looked hard at the techno-voyagers after his brief summary of the past several months, hoping to return the topic to present mode.

"Naturally, we're *grateful* for what you attempted to do out there," the commander told them now. "But good god, man, what could you have been thinking of? *One* ship against so many! Why not have waited until the rest of the Pioneer Mission arrived?"

Leonard noticed Carpenter and the navigator exchange glances and braced himself for the worst. Carpenter was looking at him gravely.

"I'm afraid you've misunderstood us, Commander," the major began. "The Pioneer Mission will not be returning. Admiral Hunter and General Reinhardt can only offer you their prayers, and their firm conviction that the fate of Earth lies in good hands, with you and the valiant defense forces under your command, sir. But expect no assistance from the SDF-3, Commander, none whatsoever."

"And may God help them," the navigator muttered under his breath.

Leonard made a sound of disapproval.

"I wonder if there'll be anyone left on Earth to appreciate their prayers by the time they return from space," Rolf said, his back to the room while he watched a dark rain begin to fall on Monument City.

CHAPTER
TWELVE

Of course, Cochran told me about the alien pilot. Emerson was a fool to believe he could keep this from me. He has no inkling of the existence of the Secret Fraternity, that one which binds great minds together, all petty loyalties be damned. . . . But I am thankful for his foolishness; it allows me a freer hand in these matters. Unfortunately, though, the pilot was moved before I could intervene. And now that I have learned his name, it is imperative that I get to him as soon as possible. If he is who I believe him to be . . . my mind reels from the possibility. In certain ways, I, Zand, am his child!

Dr. Lazlo Zand, *Event Horizon: Perspectives on Dana Sterling and the Second Robotech War*

IN THE NOW HEAVILY GUARDED LABORATORY OF Miles Cochran, the Bioroid pilot who would come to be known as Zor Prime, writhed in apparent agony, his lean but well-muscled arms straining at the ties that kept him confined to the bed. Masked and gowned, Rolf Emerson, Nova Satori, and Alan Fredericks watched with concern, while the professor monitored the captive's vital signs from the sterile room's staging area. The fine-featured young alien had come out of his coma three hours before (prompting Emerson's second predawn visit to the lab), but claimed to know nothing of his past or present circumstances.

"A most convenient case of amnesia," Fredericks suggested, breaking the uneasy silence that prevailed when Zor's cries had subsided some. "I think it's all too obvious that the creature is a mole. These so-called Robotech

Masters hope to infiltrate an agent in our midst by the most transparent of ploys. A Bioroid pilot who suddenly has no memory of his past," the GMP man scoffed. "Absurd. Not only that, but after-mission reports by the Fifteenth Tactical Armor suggest that this particular Bioroid was *deliberately* shot down by the enemy forces."

Rolf Emerson nodded his head in agreement. "I'm tempted to agree with your assessment, Colonel. Still, there are ways we can use him—"

"How do we know he isn't one of our own hostages returned to us?" Fredericks interrupted. "Perhaps the aliens have sent us a brainwashed captive simply to convince us that we're waging a war against members of our own species?"

"General," Cochran spoke up, walking into their midst with an armful of diagnostic readouts. "Excuse me, Emerson, but please allow me to present my findings before you succeed in convincing yourself this pilot is an enemy plant."

"Go ahead, Doctor," Rolf said apologetically.

Cochran ran his forefinger down the data columns of the continuous printout sheet. "Yes, here...." He cleared his throat. "Scans of the limbic system, extending along the hippocampal formation of the medial temporal lobes, fornix, and mammillary bodies, to the anterior nuclei of the thalamus, cingulum, septal area, and the orbital surface of the frontal lobes, most definitely point to diffuse cerebral impairment of the memory centers.

"It's quite unlike anything I've seen," he added, removing his glasses. "Inappropriate to classify as retrograde or anterograde, and, as it appears, only marginally posttraumatic. Closer to a fugue state than anything else, but I'd like to consult with Professor Zand before committing myself to any reductive explanation."

"Absolutely not," Emerson barked, stepping forward. "I don't want anyone else involved in this case, *least* of all Zand. Is that understood?"

Cochran gave a reluctant nod.

"Now what are our options, Doctor?" Rolf wanted to know.

Cochran replaced his eyeglasses. "Well, treatment varies with the subject, General. We might try hypnosis, of course."

"What about environmental manipulation?" Nova suggested. The GMP lieutenant looked over at the pilot. "His brain patterns are obviously abnormal, but they do appear to be stabilizing. Suppose we transferred him to another environment."

"Somewhere more *Human*, you mean," said Rolf.

"Yes."

"But who would supervise the treatment?" asked Fredericks.

"I would," Nova said confidently. "He doesn't seem to have a violent nature, and if the amnesia is genuine, he'll need someone to trust and confide in. . . ."

"It has been known to work. . . ." Cochran agreed.

"I think you're onto something, Lieutenant," Rolf said encouragingly. "But where do you suggest we bring him?"

"The base hospital," Nova answered. "We can secure a floor and gradually bring him into contact with the outside world." She gestured to the room's equipment banks and ob windows. "This place is simply too intimidating, too sterile."

"There's a reason for that," Cochran said defensively, but Emerson cut him off.

"I'm putting you in charge, Lieutenant Satori. But remember: the strictest security must be maintained."

Marie Crystal took a healthy bite out of a Red Delicious apple (from the fruit basket her squad had sent over, along with the flowers presently vased on the bedside table), and flipped through the pages of the glamour magazine she had purchased. It seemed a little bizarre—reading about projected fashion trends for the coming year when there was a war on—but she assured herself that it had probably always been thus: no matter how cruel the circumstance, the fundamental things applied. . . .

She was sitting crosslegged on the bed, the mag spread in front of her, an appealing portrait in dark-blue satin, when she heard a knock at the door.

"All right, c'mon out," a mock-stern voice threatened. "This is hospital security, and we know there's a perfectly healthy person in there."

There was no mistaking Sean's voice. She told him to wait a minute, stashed the magazine under the bed, and got back under the covers, clutching them tight to her neck and doing a reasonable impersonation of a patient.

Sean entered a moment later, flowers in hand. "Hi, Marie," he said, full of good cheer. "I thought I'd drop by and apologize for not coming sooner, but they've been keeping us pretty busy. . . . Who the heck brought you these?" he said of the squad's gift, pulling the yellow flowers from the vase and trashing them. He replaced them with his own bouquet.

Marie made a face behind his back and faked a small but agonized moan, subsiding to quiet whimpers as he turned to her.

"Hey, what's the matter?" he said, leaning over her now.

She came up hard and fast with a backhand as he was reaching out for her, slapping his arm away.

"Get away from me!" she growled into his surprised look. "What's the matter, you big jerk—you couldn't find any nurses to play with?"

Sean was open-armed, in a gesture of bewilderment. "Marie, you must have taken one on the head. I came to see *you*—"

"Just keep your hands to yourself!" she snarled, then groaned for real as a stabbing abdominal pain snuck up on her.

"My, my . . . you poor little darlin'," Sean teased. "You really are a credit to your uniform, the way you handle the *excruciating* agony. Or maybe I should say *lack* of uniform," he added, leering at her fondly.

Marie ignored the comment, not bothering to conceal her cleavage as she leaned up onto her elbows. "I'm faking it, is that it?" she said angrily.

Sean risked sitting on the edge of the bed, his hand stroking his jaw contemplatively. "No . . . Well, actually, the thought *had* crossed my mind." He folded his arms and sighed. "You know, looking back on it, I wonder what I was thinking when I *saved your life.*"

Marie's eyes narrowed. "Looking for *gratitude*, Sean?"

"Aw, come on," he smiled. "Maybe just a little friendliness, that's all."

Marie's head dropped back to the pillow, eyes on the ceiling. "This whole mess should never have happened. It's all Sterling's fault I'm lying here like a lump."

"Calm down," he told her sincerely. "You can't blame Dana."

She turned on him. "Don't tell me what I can do ground-pounder! I hate the Fifteenth—the whole bunch of you."

Sean held up his hands. "Wait a minute—"

"Get out of here!" she yelled at him, the pillow raised like a weapon now. "Out!"

He backed off and exited the room without another word, leaving her to stare at the pink roses he brought and wonder if she had overplayed her hand a bit.

In the corridor outside Marie's room, Sean bumped into Dana, a bouquet in her hand and obviously on her way to pay a visit to the Fifteenth's newest enemy. Sean stepped in front of her, blocking her advance on Marie's room with small talk.

"And if you're here to see Marie, you can forget it,"

he finally got around to saying. "The staff didn't give the okay for her to have visitors."

Dana looked suspicious. "She was admitted days ago. Besides, they let *you* see her, didn't they?"

"Uh, they made an exception for me," Sean stammered as Dana pushed her way past him. "After all, I'm the guy who—"

"Does she still hate me?" Dana asked, suddenly realizing the purpose of Sean's double-talk.

Sean's forced smile collapsed. "Even worse. She's mad enough to say that she hates *me*! It'll probably blow over," he hastened to add. "But right now she kinda considers you responsible."

"Me?! Why?" Dana pointed to herself. "Jeez, *I* didn't shoot her down!"

"We know that," Sean said reassuringly. "She's just looking for someone to blame. And if she hadn't been trying to save that Sullivan dude . . ."

"Brother. . . ." Dana sighed, shaking her head.

They were both silent for a moment; then turned together to the sound of controlled commotion at the far end of the hospital corridor. A dozen GMP soldiers, armed and armored, were supervizing the rapid transit of a stretcher to the elevator banks.

"What's all this about?" Dana wondered aloud.

"The place is crawling with Gimps," Sean told her. "I heard they cordoned off the whole ninth floor."

Dana snorted. "Leonard's probably here for his annual physical."

But even as she said it, something didn't sit well. Nonetheless, she gave a final look at the draped form on the stretcher and shrugged indifferently.

To avoid a scene like the one recently played in war room, Rolf Emerson decided it was best to inform Leonard of the new arrangements he had made for the alien pilot, who, shortly before being transferred to the base hospital, had given his name as Zor.

Zor!—the name Dana had mentioned in debriefing sessions following the rescue of Bowie at the Macross mounds. It had seemed coincidental then, but now...

Zor!

A name notorious these past fifteen years; a name whispered on the lips of everyone connected with Robotechnology; a name at once despised and held in the greatest reverence. Zor, whom the Zentraedi had credited with the discovery of Protoculture; Zor, the Tirolian scientist who had sent the SDF-1 to Earth, unwittingly ushering in the near destruction of the planet, the eclipse of the Human race.

Of course it was possible that Zor was a common name among these people called the Masters. But then again...

Emerson said as much to the commander when he reported to him. Leonard, however, was not impressed.

"I don't care what he calls himself, or whether he's Human or android," the commander growled. "All I know is that your investigation has thus far been fruitless. The man's name is no great prize, General. Not when we're after *military* data."

"Professor Cochran is confident that the change in environment will result in a breakthrough," Rolf countered.

"I want facts!" Leonard emphasized. "This Bioroid pilot is a soldier—perhaps an important one. I want him pumped for information and I frankly don't give a damn how that's accomplished."

Emerson held his ground. "All the more reason for caution at this point, Commander. His mind is fragile, which means he can either snap or become useful to us. We've got to find out what the Masters are after."

Leonard's fist came down on the desk. "Are you blind, man? It's obvious what they want—the complete obliter-

ation of the Human race! A fresh planet to use for coloni-
zation!"

"But there's the Protoculture Matrix—"

"To hell with that mystical claptrap!" Leonard bellowed, up on his feet now, hands flat on the desk. "And
to hell with caution! Bring me results, or I'll have that
pilot's head, General—to do with as *I* see fit!"

The day's rain seemed to have scoured the Earth
clean; there were even traces of redolent aromas in the
washed air, sweet smells wafting in on an evening breeze
that found Dana on the barrack's balcony. Strange to
stare at the sawtoothed ridgeline now, she said to herself,
the fortress gone but the harsh memories of its brief stay
etched in her thoughts. The recon mission, a city of
clones; then Sullivan, Marie, countless others . . . And
presiding over all of it, robbing her of sleep these past few
nights, the image of the red Bioroid pilot: his handsome,
elfin face, his long lavender-silver locks . . .

Dana closed her eyes tightly, as though in an effort to
compress the image to nothingless, atomize it somehow
and free herself. It was worse now that she had gleaned
some information about the Expeditionary Mission.

She might never see her parents again.

Silently, Bowie joined her at the balcony rail while her
eyes were shut; but she was aware of his presence and
smiled even before turning to him. They held each other's
hands without exchanging a word, drinking in the sweet
night air and the sounds of summer insects. There was
nothing that needed to be said; since their youth they had
talked about Max and Miriya, Vince and Jean, what they
would do when the SDF-3 returned, what they would do
if it never returned. They were close enough to read each
others thoughts sometimes, so it didn't surprise Dana
when Bowie mentioned the alien girl, Musica.

"I know that the fortress represents the enemy," he
said softly. "And I'm aware that I don't have much to go

on, Dana. But she's not one of them—I'm sure of it. Something went off deep in my heart . . . and suddenly I believed in her."

Dana gave his hand a reaffirming prolonged squeeze.

Was *that* what her heart was telling her about the red Bioroid pilot?—that she *believed* in him?!

He had been moved; he knew that much. This room was warmer than the first, empty of that corral of machines and devices that had surrounded him. He also knew that there were fewer eyes on him, mechanical and otherwise. His body was no longer host to that array of sensor pads and transmitters; the vein in his wrist no longer receiving the slow nutrient flow; his breathing passages unrestricted. His arms . . . *free.*

Gone, too, were the nightmares: those horrible images of the mindless attack launched against him by protoplasmic creatures; the giant warriors who somehow seemed to have been fighting on his behalf; the explosions of light and a seering pain; the death and . . . *resurrection!*

Were they nightmares or was this something recalled to life?—*something one part of him used to keep buried!*

There was a female seated in a chair at the foot of his bed. Her handsome features and jet-black hair gave her an alluring look, and yet there was something cool and distant about her that overrode the initial impression. She sat with one leg crossed over the other, a primitive writing board device in her lap. She wore a uniform and a communicatorlike headband that seemed to serve no other purpose than ornamentation. Her voice was rich and melodic, and as she spoke he recalled her from the short list of memories logged in his virgin mind, recalled her as the one who had asked questions of him earlier on, before this sleep had intervened, gently but probing. He remembered that he desired to trust her, to confide in her. But there had been precious little to tell. Other than his name . . . his *name* . . .

Zor.

"Welcome back," Nova Satori said pleasantly when she noticed Zor's eyes open. "You've been asleep."

"Yes," he said uncertainly. His mind seemed to speak it in several tongues at once, but foremost came the one the female was versed in.

"Did you dream again?" she asked.

He shook his head and raised himself up in the bed. The female—*Nova*, he remembered—motioned to a device that allowed him to raise the head portion of the padded sleeping platform. He activated it, marveling at its primitive design, and wondering why the bed wasn't reconfiguring of its own accord. Or by a prompt from his thought or will . . .

"What's the last strong impression you remember from your past?" Nova asked after a minute.

For some unknown reason, the question angered him. But with the anger returned the dream, more clearly now, and it seemed to him suddenly that at one time he had been a soldier of some sort. He told her as much, and she wrote something on her notepad.

"And after that?"

Zor searched for something in his thoughts, and said: "You."

"Nothing in between?"

Zor shrugged. Once again the dream resurfaced. Only this time it was more lucid still. His very body was participating in the memory, recalling where it stood and how it felt. And with this came a remembrance of pain.

Nova watched him slide into it and was on her feet and by his side instantly, trying to soothe him, recall him from whatever memories were driving him into such unmitigated suffering and agony. She felt a concern that ran much deeper than curiosity or nefarious purpose, and gave in to it, her hand on his fevered brow, her heart beating almost as rapidly as his.

"Let go of it, Zor," she said, her mouth close to his

ear. "Don't push yourself—it will all come back to you in time. Don't drive yourself to this!"

His back was arched, chest heaved up unnaturally. He groaned and put his hands to his head, praying for it to end.

"Make it stop," he said through clenched teeth. Then, curiously: "I promise I won't try to remember any more!"

Nova stepped back some, aware that he wasn't talking to her.

CHAPTER
THIRTEEN

He's the leader of a race of clones,
Who'd come to Earth to smash some bones.
He's the Bioroid with lots of fight,
The Disturber of your sleep at night;
He screams "Victory, bab-ee, victory!
I'm invincible, I'm somebody!"
Just get into a duel with—
the Crimson Pilot

"Crimson Pilot," music by Bowie Grant,
lyrics by Louie Nichols

DANA LEFT THE WINDOWS OF HER ROOM OPEN
that night, hoping that starlight and those redolent
aromas would provide some soporific enchantment and
ease her into sleep. But instead the light cast menacing
shadows on the wall and the smells and sounds drove her
to distraction. She tossed and turned for most of the night
and just before sunrise lapsed into a fitful sleep plagued
by nightmares that featured none other than the red
Bioroid pilot. As a result she slept late. Upon awakening,
still half in the grip of the night's fear and terror, she
literally ran to the compound's battle simulator, where
she chose land-based Bioroid combat scenario one-D-
one-niner, and exorcised her demons by annihilating a
holographic image of the crimson pilot, setting a new high
score on the mecha-sized machine.

Entering her initials to the software package, however,
was not prize enough to stabilize the circular pattern of

her thoughts, and she carried a mixture of anger and bafflement with her for the rest of the day.

Sunset found her wandering into the 15th's readyroom, where Bowie was at the piano, vamping on the atonal progression of half-notes he had heard in Musica's harp chamber and finally been able to recall (and score). Angelo, Louie, Xavez, and Marino were lounging about.

"It's good to hear you playing again," Dana complimented him. She tried to hum the curious melody. "What is that?"

"It's as close as I can get to Musica's harp," he told her, right hand running through the modulating riff again. Bowie put both hands to it now, improvising an enhancement. "What kind of people can create music like this and still find it in their hearts to kill?"

"Don't confuse the people with their leaders," Dana started to say as Sean burst into the room. He made a beeline for her and was out-of-breath when he spoke.

"Lieutenant, you're not gonna believe this, but do *I* have a piece of news!"

"Out with it," she said, without a clue.

"I did some investigating and found out who the GMP have stashed away on the ninth floor of the medical center. It's a captured Bioroid pilot—a *red* Bioroid pilot."

Dana's mouth fell open. "Did you see him?"

Sean shook his head. "They've got him under pretty tight security."

"How did you find this out, Sean?" Bowie asked from the piano stool.

Sean touched his forefinger to his nose. "Well, my friend, let's just say that it pays to make friends with a cute nurse now and again. . . ."

Dana made an impatient gesture. "Do you think it's him, Sean—*Zor*, the one we saw in the fortress?"

"Don't know," he confessed.

"I've got to see him," she said, beginning to pace.

"Those Gimps might have some different ideas about that," Sean said to her back.

"I don't care about them," Dana spat. "I've got some questions to ask, and that Bioroid pilot's the only one capable of answering them!"

"Yeah, but you'll never get to see him," Louie Nichols chimed in.

Angelo had also picked up on the conversation. "I don't know what you've got in mind, Lieutenant, but I don't think it's a good idea to stick our noses where they don't belong."

"In any case," Louie pointed out, "he's probably been programmed against divulging information. It's not likely you'll get anything out of him."

"You're probably right," Dana agreed. "But I don't think I'm going to be able to get a good night's sleep until I confront him face-to-face."

Sean put his hands on his hips and thought for a moment. "Well, if it means that much to you, then let's do it. But how are we going to get in there?"

Dana considered this, then smiled in sudden realization. "I've got an idea," she laughed; then quickly added, "Fasten your seatbelts, boys—it's going to be a bumpy night!"

An hour later, a bogus maintenance transport was rumbling through the darkened streets of Monument City en route to the medical center. Louie had the wheel. Stopped at the gate, Angelo, riding shotgun, flashed a phonied-up requisition and repair order at the sleepy guard.

"Maintenance wants us to fix a ruptured ion gun in one of your X-ray scanning sequencers," the sergeant said knowingly.

The guard scratched absently at his helmet and waved the vehicle through. As it entered the underground garage, Louie said, "'By the way, ion guns don't rupture.'"

"Rupture, shmupture," Angelo rhymed. "It got us in, didn't it?"

Louie steered the transport to a secluded parking area. Angelo hopped down from the front seat and threw open the rear doors: out stepped Bowie, Sean, Marino, and Xavez—all in coveralls and visored caps—and Dana, in a nurse's uniform that was at least three sizes too small for her and fit her like a second skin. Louie and Bowie immediately began toying with the hospital's phone and com line switches, while the rest of the men started to strip down. . . .

In Zor's ninth floor room, Nova put her clipboard aside to answer the phone. A nasal voice at the other end said:

"This is the office of Chief-of-Staff Emerson, Lieutenant Satori, and the general requests that you meet with him at the Ministry as soon as possible."

Nova frowned at the handset and recradled it. She apologized to Zor for having to leave so suddenly, and a minute later was on her way. . . .

Bowie, who had a reputation for vocal impressions, unpinched his nose and informed the team that Satori had taken the bait. The coveralls gone now, Angelo wore bedroom slippers and an unremarkable cotton terry robe. Marino and Xavez were dressed like orderlies. Sean was in his usual uniform.

"Okay," Dana told the sergeant, "make your move in ten minutes."

"I never missed a cue," Angelo promised.

Nova told the two GMP guards who were stationed either side of the door to Zor's room to keep their eyes peeled.

"I'll be back shortly," she said.

At the same time, someone pushed the buzzer outside Marie Crystal's seventh floor room. She was sitting in bed, reading a bodybuilding magazine, which she quickly hid from sight, slipping beneath the sheets as she did so and feigning sleep.

A moment later, the doors hissed open and in walked Sean.

Marie sat up, surprised. "What are you doing here at this time of night?"

Meanwhile, on the ground floor, Dana, toting a large shoulderbag (her nurse's cap in place), was escorting a stretcher to one of the elevators; the stretcher was borne by Xavez and Marino, both wearing surgical masks—to hide their smiles as much as anything else. They entered the car, pushing seven on the floor display, just as the adjacent elevator opened, allowing Nova Satori to step out.

Upstairs, Sean was down on one knee at Marie's bedside. "I got to thinking . . . you lying here all by yourself. I was worried about you."

"Oh, no kidding," she returned sarcastically.

"Seriously," he persisted. "It's a beautiful night, Marie. And I thought you might like to go up on the roof and enjoy it with me. A change of scenery, you know?"

Marie laughed. "Sounds great, but these doctors watch every move I make."

Sean stood up and lowered his voice conspiratorially. "How 'bout if I promised you you wouldn't get in any trouble?"

She threw him a puzzled look.

"I cleared it all with the administration," he said with elaborate innocence.

Marie couldn't help but be a little suspicious. "Why me, Sean?"

"Because you're so sweet and gentle," he flattered her. "I can't help myself!" Then all at once there was a light rap at the door and he seemed suddenly impatient. "Come on, get ready. Your limousine's here."

No sooner had Marie run a hand through her hair and

cinched her robe, than the doors hissed open again. Two masked orderlies appeared bearing a stretcher.

Marie leaned back, startled and having second thoughts. "Sean, I don't know about this. . . ."

"What's the matter?" he said, coming over to the bed. "Let's not look a gift horse in the mouth." Without warning he pulled back the bed covers, and a second later, Marie found herself in his arms, being carried over to the waiting stretcher and those grinning orderlies. . . .

As soon as the 15th's trio had conveyed the stretcher a safe distance down the deserted corridor, Dana raced into Marie's room, doffed the starched cap, and opened the window. She leaned out and looked up: Zor's room was two stories directly above. From the shoulder bag, she retrieved a stun gun, a short coil of rope, and four climber's suction cups. She put her arm through the former, and strapped the cups to her knees and wrists. She tucked the stun gun into the uniform's narrow belt. That much accomplished, she climbed up on to the window stool and commenced her fly-crawl up the marble side of the building.

Reaching the ninth floor, she peered cautiously into the window, almost losing her grip when she saw Zor, the crimson pilot, sitting in the room's single bed, a uniform jacket over his shoulders. She lowered herself down when he seemed to sense her presence and turned to the window. She stayed that way for several seconds, then checked her watch. It read 9:29.

"Almost time," she said quietly, fixing a rope to the window's exterior frame. . . .

At exactly 9:30 a slippered and bathrobed Sergeant Dante stepped from one of the ninth floor elevators. Three GMP sentries were on him immediately.

"Get back in the elevator," one of them told him curtly. "This floor's closed to the public."

Angelo waited for the doors to close and then said:

"That's all right, I'm allowed to be up here." He began to walk off nonchalantly. A second guard restrained him.

"Check this guy out with security," the guard ordered one of his companions. The man ran to the wall phone, but reported back with a shout that the line was dead.

Thanks to Louie's basement tampering, Dante thought.

"Lemme go, you guys," the sergeant protested to the two who had taken hold of his arms. "I tell ya, I'm here to see my wife!"

"Simmer down, pal," said the one on Dante's left. "We're going to go for a little walk. You coming quietly or do we have to drag you?"

Dante smiled inwardly and prepared himself for battle. . . .

In his room a short distance down the corridor, Zor heard the commotion and got out of bed to investigate. It was all the diversion Dana needed: she leapt in through the window, her stun gun in hand.

"Stop right there!" she told Zor, who was just short of the door.

Zor turned and began to walk toward her, wordless but determined.

"Stay back!" Dana warned him, arming the gun and bringing both hands to the grip. "If you don't stop, I'll fire!"

But he was undeterred, one moment stalking her, and the next three feet over her head in a superleap that brought him down precisely on the gun. As it flew from her hands, Dana dropped back, adopting a defensive pose and waiting for him to come.

Zor leaned forward as if to step, but ducked adroitly as she came around with a roundhouse right. He threw himself against her midsection, taking her down easily and pinning her to the floor, his left hand clamped on her left wrist, his right forearm pressed to her throat, firm enough to strangle the breath from her.

"Why are you trying to kill me?" he demanded. "What have I done?!"

Dana gasped for air, managing to say: "You're responsible for killing men under my command!" *And more!*

She saw his eyes go wide in surprise, felt the pressure against her trachea lessen, and made the most of it, heaving up with her legs and throwing him over her head. But the nimble alien landed on his feet after a back flip, combat-crouched as Dana moved in on him.

He avoided her side kick and dropped to the floor, sweeping Dana's legs out from under her with his right foot. She came down hard on the side of her face and lost it for a moment. When she looked up, the alien had the gun trained on her.

"You're the one," Dana said, struggling to her feet. "The red Bioroid."

"What are you saying?!" He questioned her.

Dana had her fists clenched, her feet spread for another kata. "You're the one we saw at the mounds—the one who captured Bowie! And the one in the fortress!"

Zor relaxed his gun hand somewhat, his face betraying the bewilderment he felt. "Nova told me the same thing," he said with troubled brow. "What does it mean—*Bioroid*?"

Dana straightened from her pose. "Your memory only works when you're killing my men, is that it?!" she shouted. "I don't know why I'm even bothering with you, *alien*!"

Zor winced as though kicked. "Alien?" he seemed to ask himself; then: "I'm a Human being!"

Which he barely got out: Dana's powerful front kick caught him square on the chin and slammed him back against the wall. He still had the gun, but it was now hanging absently by his side.

"I was there when you crawled out of that Bioroid!" Dana seethed. "Don't deny it!" She stood waiting for him to get up, her hands ready; but the alien remained on his knees, blood running from his mouth.

"I won't," he said contritely. "But I wasn't responsible for what I was doing." Zor looked at her and said: "You've got to believe me!"

"Who made you do it?! Who are they?!" Dana demanded.

Resigned, Zor threw the gun at her feet. "Can't you see?" he said, full of self-disgust. "I've lost my memory. . . ."

Back at the elevators, Bowie Grant, in a white coat as large on him as Dana's nurse's uniform was small, had come to Angie's assistance. Not that the sergeant needed any: one guard was already unconscious, the one gripped in Dante's left arm well on the way, and the third was more than halfway there. Somehow, all of them had lost their helmets in the struggle.

"Ah, excuse me, Mr. Campbell," Bowie was saying in his best professorial voice. "Your wife's room is on the *eighth* floor."

Dante tossed the two sentries aside dismissively and went on to finish his scene with Bowie, playing to an all but unconscious house.

"So I made a mistake, Doc—is that any reason for these gorillas of yours to jump down my throat?!"

Bowie, too, was willing to play along, especially now that the three were coming around. "Calm down, Mr. Campbell. They were only doing their job. And you can hardly blame them for that, right?"

Angelo laughed shortly and let a whistling Bowie lead him away. . . .

The tune Bowie whistled was a strange one, with an unusual but haunting melody. It was Dana's signal to make her escape. She said as much to Zor who was now seated on the edge of the bed, his head in his hands.

"You can't remember anything at all?" Dana asked one final time.

"No, it's hopeless," Zor started to say but suddenly looked up at the sound of the whistled tune. "That music," he said anxiously. "What is that music?!"

Dana knelt beside him. "One of my troopers learned it from an alien girl on the fortress," she explained.

"Yes . . . I *remember*!" Zor exclaimed. "A girl named . . . *Musica*."

Dana gasped. "That's right!" *So Bowie's vision was real after all,* she said to herself.

"I'm not even certain how I know that," Zor shrugged. . . .

Elsewhere, Lieutenant Nova Satori was storming back to the med center elevators. "No one makes a fool out of me like that!" she seethed out loud when the car doors closed. . . .

"But this is great!" Dana was telling the alien, no longer anxious to leave the room. "It's starting to look like your memory's returning!"

Zor shook his head in despair.

And suddenly the doors hissed open.

Dana thought it might be Bowie and Angelo, but when she turned she found Nova Satori glaring at her.

"I'll have your bars for this, Sterling!" she heard the GMP lieutenant say. Dana took two quick steps and launched herself out the window, rappeling down to Marie's room with Nova's threats ringing in her ears.

CHAPTER
FOURTEEN

Ironically, the man who could have helped most was also the one who could have done the most damage—Dr. Lazlo Zand, who emerges from his own works and those of numerous commentators as a kind of voyeur to Earth's ravaging by the Robotech Masters. His pathological manipulation of Dana Sterling has only recently come to light [see Zand's own Event Horizon*] and one understands completely why Major General Rolf Emerson was loath to involve the scientist in any of Earth's dealings with its new invaders. But it must be pointed out that only Zand, Lang's chief disciple, could have provided the answers to the questions Earth Command was asking. It is indeed fascinating to speculate what might have come from a meeting between Zand and Zor Prime.*

Zeitgeist, *Insights: Alien Psychology and the Second Robotech War*

NOVA'S FIRST THOUGHT WAS TO HAVE DANA AR-rested by the GMP for knowingly violating security, tampering, or whatever trumped-up charges the boys at dirty tricks could dream up. But the fact remained that Dana's encounter with Zor had resulted in a breakthrough of sorts. When Nova had questioned him after Dana's swashbuckling escape from the ninth floor hospital room, it was evident that something within the alien had been stirred; he had at least partial recall of names and faces apparently linked to his recent past, perhaps while on-board the alien fortress itself.

Professor Cochran was already revising his initial diagnosis based on Nova's updated report; he was now rejecting the idea of fugue state and thinking more in terms of the retrograde type, or possibly a novel form of transient global amnesia. Brain scans done after the alien's fight with Lieutenant Sterling indicated that the limbic abnormalities detected earlier had lessened to some degree; but Cochran was still in the dark as to the etiology. He pressed Nova to openly call in Professor Zand, but Nova refused; she promised him, however, that she would make mention of Zand during her meeting with General Emerson.

The general was furious with Sterling for about five minutes. After that, Nova could see that a new plan had come to him, one that would place Dana Sterling at the very center of things. Nova would retain control over Zor's debriefing, but Dana was to provide the stimulus.

Emerson explained all this to Dana scarcely a week after the med center players had made chumps out of the GMP sentries.

Dana hadn't heard word one from Nova or High Command during that time and had spent her idle moments preparing herself for the brig, working her body to exhaustion in the barracks workout rooms, and trying to make some sense out of the conflicting emotions she now felt toward the alien pilot. Zor had been spirited away from the base hospital and even Sean hadn't been able to pry any additional information from the nursing staff.

So Dana was hardly surprised when the call came for her to report to General Emerson at the Ministry. But there were surprises in store for her she couldn't have guessed at.

Rolf was seated rigidly at his desk when Dana announced herself and walked into the spacious office. Colonel Rochelle was standing off to one side, *Zor* to the other. Dana offered a salute and Rolf told her in a scolding voice to step up to the desk.

"I suppose there's no need for me to introduce you to Zor, Lieutenant Sterling. It is my understanding that *you two have already met.*"

Dana gulped and said, "Yes, sir. You see—"

"I don't want to hear your explanations, Dana," Rolf interrupted, waving his hand dismissively. "This issue's confused enough already." He cleared his throat meaningfully. "What you may or may not know, is that Zor is apparently amnesiac—either as a result of the crash or perhaps through some neural safeguard the Masters saw fit to include in their Human pilots. Nevertheless, it is our belief that he can be brought through this. In fact, your previous . . . *encounter* with him seems to have provided a start in that direction."

"Uh, thank you, sir," Dana muttered, instantly wishing she could take it back. Rolf's eyes were flashing with anger.

"Don't *thank* me, Lieutenant! What you did was unconscionable, and at some point you'll be expected to make amends for it!" Rolf snorted. "But for the time being, I want to place Zor under your personal direction. I want him to take part in the Fifteenth's activities."

Dana was aghast. "Sir? . . . Do you mean? . . ." She looked over at Zor, struck by how terrific he looked in the uniform and boots someone had supplied him: a tight-fitting navy blue and scarlet jumpsuit, cinched by a wide, gold-colored belt, and turtle-necked, making his lavender locks appear even longer. His faint smile brought a similar one to her face.

"I think I understand the logic here," she said, turning back to Rolf. "A military assignment may jog his memory in some way."

"Precisely," said Rolf. "Do you think you can handle it, Dana?"

Again she looked over at Zor; then nodded. "I'm willing to try, sir."

"And what about your team?"

Dana thought her words out carefully before speaking. "The Fifteenth is the finest unit in the Southern Cross, sir. Everyone will do their part."

"And Bowie?"

Dana's lips tightened. Bowie would be harder to handle. "I'll talk to him," she told Rolf. "He'll come through, and I'm willing to stake my bars on it."

Emerson looked hard at her and said, "You are, Lieutenant."

When Dana had left the room with Zor, Colonel Rochelle had some things to say to Emerson, starting off by disavowing the entire project. "It's insane," he told Rolf, gesticulating as he paced in front of the desk. "And I want no further part of it. An alien pilot—an *officer*, at that—wandering around with one of our top units. . . . Suppose he *is* a mole? Suppose he's wired or rigged in some way we can't even fathom? We might just as well give the Masters an open invitation to have a peek at our defenses."

Emerson let him speak; Rochelle wasn't saying anything that Rolf hadn't already thought, feared, scrutinized, and analyzed to death.

"And why Sterling? She's a discipline problem and a—"

Rochelle cut himself off short of the word, but Emerson finished the thought for him.

"That's right, Colonel. She's half-alien herself. Part Human, part Zentraedi, and therefore the perfect choice in this instance." Rolf exhaled loudly, tiredly. "I know full well how risky this is. But this Zor is our only hope. If we can show him who we are, then perhaps he can become our voice to the Masters. If they're after what I *think* they're after, we've got to use Zor to convince them that we don't have it."

"The legendary Protoculture factory," Rochelle said knowingly. "I just hope you know what you're doing, sir."

Eyes closed, Emerson leaned back in his chair and said nothing.

"Our new recruit's a very skilled soldier," Dana told the assembled members of the 15th. "I can tell you that he was assigned to us personally by General Emerson himself, and that I have the utmost confidence in him."

The team, including a couple of greens fresh from the Academy, was gathered at ease in the barracks ready-room. Dana had been building up the new recruit for the past five minutes and Angelo for one was beginning to get suspicious. Especially with all this talk about having faith enough in the decision of High Command to accept a mission that seems somewhat extraordinary on the face of it.

"All right, you can come in now," the lieutenant was saying, half-turned to the ready-room sliders.

The doors hissed open and the lean, clean-shaven recruit entered. He was handsome in an almost androgynous way, above-average height, and affected a shade of light purple dye in his long hair. The yoke and flyout shoulders of his uniform were green to Dana's red, the cadets' yellow, and Louie's blue. Dana introduced him as Zor.

The name had no meaning to some of them, but Angelo gave loud voice to the sudden concerns of the rest.

"Is this *the alien*?!"

Dana said, "Zor is officially part of our unit."

Now everyone went bananas—all except Bowie, who Dana had spoken to beforehand and who was now gritting his teeth. Murmurs of disbelief and confusion swept through the ranks, until Dante angrily called them to a halt.

"Lieutenant, is this the real dope?" Corporal Nichols asked unconvinced.

"Blazing Battloids," Dana responded. "Do you think I'm making this *up*?"

Again the comments began and again Dante silenced them, stepping forward this time and fixing Zor with a gimlet stare.

"Lieutenant, I saw this alien *shot down by his own troops*! I saw it with my *own* eyes! The guy's a spy! What is it—too *obvious* for High Command to see that?! He's a damn *spy*!"

"No way I want him for *my* wingman," Sean called out.

"QUIET!" Dana shouted as things began to escalate.

"Now, I'm still in command here, and I'm telling you that Zor is *officially* assigned to our unit! You let the general staff worry about whether or not he's a spy. It's our job to make him feel welcome and that's the long and short of it!" Dana stood, arms akimbo, with her chin thrust forward. "Any questions?" When no one spoke, she said: "Dismissed!"

All but Louie Nichols began filing out of the room, throwing hostile stares at the new recruit. The corporal, though, went over to Zor and extended his hand.

"Welcome to the Fifteenth," Louie said sincerely.

Zor accepted the proffered hand haltingly. It was easy enough to see where most of the team stood; but what was he supposed to feel toward those who were suddenly befriending him?

"So, big fella," Louie smiled. "You and Dana—you two getting along all right?"

The situation was, of course, *fascinating* to Nichols: the child of a bio-genetically engineered XT and a Human, now made responsible for an XT who might very well have contributed his own cellular stuff to the genetic slushpile. . . . Dana and Zor could be father and daughter, sister and brother, the possibilities were limitless. But what intrigued Louie even more was the idea that this *Zor* was related in some way to his Tirolian namesake— the genius who had discovered *Protoculture* itself!

The recruit Zor was puzzled by Louie's question; but Dana seemed to have seen through the corporal's friendly gesture.

"Don't you have something better to do?" she said leadingly. "Perhaps down in the mechanics bays or something?"

Louie took the hint and smiled. "Guess I could find *something* to do. . . . Later, Dana."

"And I'll thank you to address me in the proper manner from now on!" she barked as he was backing off.

Louie reached the sliding doors just ahead of Eddie

Jordon, the younger brother of the private who had met such a cruel end during the fortress recon mission. Dana noticed the cadet add his own hostile glare to the pool before exiting, fixing Zor with a look that could kill.

They placed him in a small room, empty save for a single chair and dark save for the meager red light of a solitary filament bulb. It was all so *alien* to him: these encounters, events and challenges. And yet one part of his mind was surely familiar with it all, directing him unthinkingly through the motions, putting words in his mouth, summoning emotions and reactions. But he was aware of the absence of connection, the absence of memories that should have been tied to these same encounters and emotions. A reservoir that had been drained, which they now hoped to refill.

Taken from the room he was left alone in the dark, although his senses told him that this area was much larger than the last, and that he was under observation. The slight one who had escorted him to this new darkness had strapped a weapon on him, an unused laser pistol that somehow felt primitive and archaic in his grip. Again, the thought assaulted him that there was a kind of mindless redundancy at work here: *the weapon ought to be firing of its own accord*, adapting itself to his will, *reconfiguring....*

But all at once a spotlight found him, and he was no longer alone but at the center of a whirling ring of sequenced targets; and he understood that the nature of the test was to destroy each of these within a predetermined interval of time. Commands and countdowns were conveyed to him over an amplified address system he could not see, loud enough for him to hear through the padded silencers which someone had thought to place over his ears.

The black and white targets had been whirling faster and faster, but were now dispersing, abandoning the tight order of the circle for the safety of random, chaotic movement. A digital chronometer flashed in the background.

He spread his legs and clasped the weapon in both hands, empty of all thought and centered on picking out the sequenced target. As number one came in behind him, he crouched, turned, and squeezed off a charge, disintegrating the substanceless thing in a fiery flash. Number two flew in from his right and he holed it likewise, remaining in place for numbers three and four.

He risked a gaze at the numerical countdown and realized that he would have to press himself harder if he was to destroy all of them. His next blast took out two at once.

Now they were coming at him on edge, but still his aim proved true, as two, then three more targets were splintered and destroyed. He took out the final one with an overhead shot just as the countdown reached zero-zero-zero-zero.

As the room's overhead lights came on, Zor holstered the pistol and removed the safety muffs. Dana came running out of the control booth, complimenting Zor on his score. Behind her, were several members of the 15th, sullen looks on their faces.

"I can't believe it!" Dana was gushing. "Where did you learn to shoot like that? You beat the simulator! No one's ever done that before! You're good, Zor; you're *really* good!"

Zor felt something akin to pride but said nothing. He heard one of the cadets say, "Yeah, too good."

He was young, on the small side, with dark brown bangs and an immature but not unpleasant face. He had his arms folded across his chest, defiantly.

Eddie, Zor recalled.

"You can shoot all right, but what now, hot shot? You gonna destroy the Bioroids or us?"

Zor remained silent, uncertain.

"Can't hear you, big man!" Eddie taunted him. "What's the matter—cat got your tongue, tough guy?"

"Come on, Eddie," said Dana. "Lay off."

"*You* come on, Lieutenant!" the youth told her. "I don't buy this lost memory crap!"

Without warning Eddie drew his sidearm and leveled it at Zor, who stood motionless, almost indifferent. Dana had stepped in front of him, warning Eddie to put the gun away.

Instead the cadet grinned, said, "Here!", and gave the gun a sideways toss. Dana ducked, stumbling into Angelo's arms, and Zor caught the thing.

"And I don't think he's so tough, either!" Eddie said, walking away from all of them.

Dana drew herself upright and stared after him, hands on her hips. "Wise guy!" she muttered.

Zor looked down at the weapon, feeling a sudden revulsion.

The alien remained the outcast, but most of the 15th grudgingly grew to accept him. It seemed unlikely that he would ever be accepted as one of the team, but by and large the hostile looks had ceased. Except for Bowie and Louie, they all simply ignored him. Dana was a special case; her interest in Zor was certainly beyond the call of duty and especially worrisome to Sergeant Dante. There wasn't much he could do about it, but he kept his eyes on Zor whenever he could, still convinced that the Bioroid pilot was an agent of the Robotech Masters, and that this amnesia thing was spurious at best.

Only Sean was neutral on the issue of Dana's infatuation. It wasn't as if he hadn't given it any thought; it was just that he was too wrapped up in his own infatuation with Marie Crystal to pay it any mind. Ever since the night on the med center roof, Sean had been preoccupied with the raven-haired lieutenant, almost to the point of forgetting entirely about the other women in his life.

On the day Marie was due to be released from the hospital, Sean decked himself out in his fanciest suit and wiped the base florist clean of bouquets. He was on his way to see her, when Dana almost bowled him down in the barracks corridor. Sterling, too, was dressed to the nines: a skirt and blouse of pink shades, a white silk scarf knotted around her neck.

"Now listen, trooper," she laughed, "Marie's not going to be as easy as shooting down skylarks, do you get me?" She emphasized this by flicking her forefinger against one of the half-dozen bouquets he was carrying, shattering the petals from a rose blossom.

"Don't kid yourself," he joked back. "I shoot pretty well. . . . And what's with the civvies?" he said, giving her the once-over.

"Just a debriefing session with Zor," Dana told him, starry-eyed.

"Debriefing? In those clothes?"

"Yep," she nodded, checking her watch. "And I'm late! So tell Marie I said hi, and that I'll come and see her as soon as I can!"

With that, Dana was gone, leaving Sean to mutter in her wake: "A true space cadet."

Dana's idea of a debriefing session was to take Zor to Arcadia, Monument City's one and only amusement park. There they ate the usual junk food and fed credits to the usual games, but only Dana was interested in going on the rides. Zor watched her from the sidelines, as she allowed herself to be turned in circles in an endless variety of ways—upside-down here, centrifugally there, backwards, forwards, and sideways.

It amazed Zor that after all this she could still retain an appetite for the gooey sweets she favored; but then again, there was so much that was *uncommon* about her. At times he felt as though he knew her in some forgotten past that predated life itself, and was not so much a part of his amnesiac state, but had more to do with mystical links and occult correspondences.

For Dana it was much the same, only more so (as all

things were with her). She recognized her infatuation and did nothing to repress or disguise it. Zor was supposed to be treated openly and honestly, and Dana didn't see why love couldn't jog his memory just as well as war might. On strict orders from General Emerson, she had yet to tell him of her mixed ancestry; but given his condition, the confession would have little impact in any case. So she simply tried to keep things fun.

At one point he suggested that they return to the base, but she vetoed it, pointing out to him that *she* was the one who was in charge.

"But I'm the one you're experimenting on!" he told her, making that sad face that made her want to hold and love him. In return, he caught the look on her face and asked if something was wrong with her.

"I think I'm in love," she sighed, only to hear him respond: "That word has no meaning for me."

It was a line she had heard often enough in the past; so she lightened up at once and convinced him to at least ride the Space Tunnel with her. He wasn't wild about the idea, but ultimately relented.

The Space Tunnel was Arcadia's main attraction; prospective dare-devils were not only required to measure up to a height line but practically submit a note from their physicians as well. It was a high-speed, grueling roller-coaster ride through tunnels that had been designed to play dangerous tricks with the optic and auditory senses. Riders found themselves harnessed side-by-side into two-person antigrav cars that were hurled into a phantasmagoric session with motion sickness and pure fright.

After Zor was made to understand that Dana's screams were the result of exhilaration and not terror, he, too, began to surrender to the experience. It was only when they entered the infamous swirling-disc tunnel that things started to come apart.

There was something about the placement of those light discs along the tunnel walls, something about their vaguely oval shape and curious concavity that elicited a fearful memory . . . one he could not connect to anything but horror and capture. It seemed to tug at the very fabric of his mind, rending open places better left sealed and forgotten. . . .

Dana saw his distress and desperately tried to reach for him; but she was held fast by both gee-forces and the harness mechanism itself. She could do nothing about the former but wait for a calmer point along the course; so in the meantime she went to work on the harness, pulling the couplers free of their sockets. Almost immediately she realized she had miscalculated: the car was accelerating into a full rollover and in an instant the shoulder harness was undone and she was thrown from the seat.

Zor saw her propelled to the rear of the speeding car, the shocking sight strong enough to overcome memory's hold. Except that it wasn't only Dana that he reached out for after he'd undone his own harness, but the radiant image of a woman from his past, a gauzy pink image of love and loss, not easily forgotten in this or any other lifetime.

Zor wrestled with the image of the woman for several days. He didn't mention it to Dana or Nova Satori, but it accompanied him wherever he went, his first clear-cut memory, seemingly a key to that Pandora's Box stored in his mind.

He was with the GMP lieutenant now, viewing a series of video images that were apparently supposed to have some meaning for him, but had thus far proven less than evocative. Tall fruit-bearing trees of some kind, tendrils wrapped around an eerily luminescent globe; protoplasmic vacuoles free-floating amidst a neurallike plexus of cables and crossovers; a round-topped armored cone rising from the equally armored surface of a galactic fortress . . .

"We've been over and over these tapes, Zor," Nova said, illuminating the room with the tap of a switch. "What are you trying to do—drive us both crazy?"

Zor made a disgruntled sound. "I'm getting closer each time I look at these things. I can feel it, I can just *feel* it. I'm going to remember. *Something*, at least. I'll break through." Zor stroked his forehead absently, while Nova loaded a video cassette into a second machine. "Let's take a look at that first program again."

"What happens if you *do* regain your memory?" Nova asked him coolly. "Do you crack up or what?"

"Who would care, anyway?" Zor threw back.

Nova smiled wryly. "Maybe Dana, but she's about the only one."

The GMP lieutenant's attitude toward the alien had changed, although Zor was at a loss to understand it. He sensed that it had something to do with Dana, but didn't see how that might explain her sudden turnabout.

"Just play the tape," he told her harshly.

A red bipedal war machine Satori had called a Bioroid; other war machines in combat with Hovercrafts; *three identical mesas, round and steep-sided, crowned with vegetation and rising abruptly from a forested plain . . .*

Zor stared at the scene, a sharp pain piercing his skull, words in an ancient voice filling his inner ears.

"Earth is the final source of Protoculture," the voice began. *"The basis of our power, the life's-blood of our existence. Our foremost goal is to control this life-source by recapturing that which was stolen from us, that which was hidden from us, that which we alone are deserving of and entitled to. . . ."*

Zor was on his feet, unaware of Nova's voiced concern. He saw three shadowy shapes arise from the mounds and disappear—creatures deliberately revealing themselves for his benefit.

Nova heard him groan, then scream in agony as he collapsed unconscious across the tabletop.

Professor Cochran was unavailable and Professor Zand was tabu; so Nova had to call in a relatively low-level GS physician on loan to the GMP from the defense department.

Zor was unconscious, though not comatose, writhing on the bed Nova and the doctor had carried him to in the military police barracks.

Dr. Katz and Lieutenant Satori were standing over him now; the doctor professionally aloof and Nova encouraged by the breakthrough but at the same time alarmed. Katz had undressed Zor and given him a sedative, powerful enough to calm the alien some but not strong enough to control the unseen horrors he was experiencing.

"Earth," Zor was groaning. "Earth, Earth is the source. . . . Earth! . . . Protoculture! We must have it! . . ."

"He's finally remembering," Nova said quietly.

Katz adjusted his eyeglasses and took a final glance at the bedside charts. "There is no apparent sign of brain damage. The sedative should take effect soon and last through the night."

Nova thanked him. "One more thing," she told him before he left the room. "You are now under top-security restriction. You haven't been here at all, you've never seen this patient. Is that understood?"

"Completely," said Katz.

Nova brushed wet bangs from Zor's feverish brow and followed the doctor out.

A minute after the door closed behind her, an electrical charge seemed to take charge of the sedated alien, starting in his head and radiating out along afferent pathways, forcing his body into a kind of involuntary stiff-armed salute. Zor screamed and clutched at the bed covers, his back arched, chest heaved up, but Nova and Katz were too far away to hear him.

CHAPTER
FIFTEEN

Zor had sacrificed his life while attempting to redress some of the injustices his discoveries had brought about. It must have occurred to the Masters that his clone—properly nurtured, properly controlled to mimic the behavior of his parent/ twin—would share the same selfless qualities. Just what the Masters had planned for Zor Prime after he'd led them to the Protoculture matrix is, and forever shall be, open to speculation.

Mingta, Protoculture: Journey Beyond Mecha

IN THE ROBOTECH FLAGSHIP, STILL HOLDING IN GEO-synchronous orbit above Earth's equator, the three Masters were seated for a change. A spherical holo-field dominated the center of the triangle formed by their high-backed chairs, and in the field itself flashed enhanced video images of the world through the eyes of their agent, Zor Prime, electronic transcriptions of the data returned to them via the neural sensor implanted in the clone's brain.

"The poor blind fools actually believe they've captured a brainwashed Human," Bowkaz said acidly. "I expect the destruction of such a species will be no great loss to the galaxy."

Shaizan agreed, as an Arcadia image of thrill-seeking Dana appeared in the field. "They're like insects, but with emotions. Primitive, industrious, and productive, but frivolous. This immature female, for example...."

"Hard to believe she's an officer," he continued, light

from the holo-field sphere white-washing his aged face. "A commander of men and machines, leading them into war. . . ."

Another view of Dana now, as she appeared when scated opposite Zor at one of the park's picnic tables.

"And it seems that she is part Zentraedi," said Bowkaz, his chin resting on his hand.

Shaizan grunted meaningfully. "It doesn't seem possible, and yet the sensors have detected certain bio-genetic traits. But the mating of a Zentraedi and a Human . . . how very odd."

"The clone has sensed something in this halfbreed, and that recognition has aroused him. Emotion is obviously the key to bringing back the memories of the donor Zor."

Again the sphere image de-rezzed, only to be replaced with those scenes Nova had recently shown Zor: the red Bioroid, battling mecha, and the three mounds.

"It is no wonder the clone experienced such agony," Dag commented, referring to this last holo-projection.

Under the man-made mounds were buried the remains of the SDF-1 and -2, along with Khyron's warship. The Masters felt certain that the Protoculture matrix was intact under one of these, and had gone so far as to investigate their hunch, but were stopped cold by the wraiths who guarded the device. The clone, of course, had led that particular operation.

"The clone is regaining his donor's memory of Protoculture," Bowkaz added knowingly. "Is it possible that he will tell them what he knows? Remember how he deceived us so many years ago; we must proceed with caution."

The sphere was a sky-blue vacuum now, a portrait of empty consciousness itself, interrupted at intervals by jagged eruptions of neural activity.

"Are you suggesting that we assume control of the clone?" Shaizan asked.

Bowkaz gave a slow nod, as one final image filled the

sphere: the hostile faces of the 15th when Zor had first been introduced to them. "To avoid the risk of his being subjected to even more base emotions. I propose we begin immediately, if only to focus his mind on the Protoculture."

"Agreed," the other Masters said after a moment.

Nova's updated reports to General Emerson concerning Zor's identification with the Macross mounds and his ravings about Protoculture convinced Rolf that it was time to open up the case to the general staff. Commander Leonard agreed and an ad hoc interagency session was convened in the Ministry's committee room.

Emerson briefed the officers, and Leonard took it from there.

"The alien's flashes of memory tell us one thing: Earth is the remaining source of all Protoculture. If we can believe it, then this is the sole reason the Robotech Masters have not destroyed the planet."

No one at the table needed to be reminded that Protoculture had spared the SDF-1 from the Zentraedi in a similar fashion.

"But they will continue their attacks until they have accumulated every supply of Protoculture we have," Leonard continued. "This means that once they learn that the so-called factory was nothing but a legend, they will go after our power plants, our mecha, every Robotech device that relies on Protoculture.

"Therefore, our only hope for survival is very simple: we must attack first and make it count."

Rolf couldn't believe his ears. The idiot was right back where they were before Zor had even entered the picture.

"But Supreme Commander," he objected. "Why *provoke* an attack when we have something they would barter to get? Let's tell them we know why they're here and make a deal." Rolf raised his voice a notch to cut through the protests his proposal had elicited. "Zor can speak for us! We could get the word to them that we are open to negotiation!"

"Are you serious, General?" said Major Kinski, speaking for several of the others. "What do you propose to do—sit down and have a luncheon with the Robotech Masters?" He waved his fist at Emerson. "They won't deal; they haven't even made an attempt to communicate!"

Leonard sat quietly, recalling the personal warning the Masters had sent his way not long ago. . . .

"I'm quite serious," Rolf was responding, his hands flat on the table. "And don't raise a fist at me, young man! Now, sit down and keep quiet!"

"You heard him," Rochelle said to Kinski, backing Emerson up.

Now it was Leonard's turn to cut through the protests.

"We're not in the deal-making business, gentlemen," he said stonily. "We're here to protect the sovereignty of our planet."

"How can you even *think* of negotiating with these murderous aliens?" asked the officer on Kinski's left.

Kinski's own fist struck the table. "A military solution is the only response. Our people expect nothing less of us."

Rolf laughed maniacally, in disbelief. "Yes, they *expect* us to bring the planet to the brink once more—"

"That's enough!" Leonard bellowed, putting an end to the arguments. "We begin coordinating attack plans immediately. This session is adjourned."

Emerson and Rochelle kept their seats as the others filed out.

Zor spent four days in the hands of the GMP and was then released to rejoin the 15th. Louie Nichols greeted him warmly when he was returned to the barracks compound, desperate to show him the scale replica of the red Bioroid he had finally completed.

"I made it myself," Louie said proudly. "It's just like the one you wore in battle."

Zor stared at the thing absently and pushed his way past Louie. "I . . . don't quite remember," he said gruffly.

"Hey, what's up?" Louie insisted, catching up with him. "I'm only trying to help you remember what happened out there, buddy."

"Sure," Zor mumbled back, moving on.

Louie would have said more, but Eddie Jordon had leapt off the couch and was suddenly beside him, pulling the metal head off the replica.

"Not so fast, hot shot," Eddie yelled. "I want to talk to you. Turn around!"

Zor stopped and faced him; Eddie was hefting the heavy object, tossing it up with one hand, threateningly. Louie tried to intervene, but the cadet shoved him aside.

"You're the cause of my brother's death!" Eddie declared angrily. "You're a liar if you tell me you don't remember! Now admit it, *clone*!"

Angelo Dante was up on his feet now, warily approaching Eddie from behind.

"Come on, Zor!" Eddie hissed into Zor's face, the robot head still in his head. "Tell me—just how much did my brother suffer?!"

Zor said nothing, meeting Eddie's gaze with eyes empty of feeling, ready to accept whatever it was the cadet saw fit to deliver.

"You tell me about it!" Eddie was saying, angry but shaken; taken over by the memory of loss and now powerless against it. "I know you remember," he sobbed. "I just want to . . ."

Eddie's head was bowed, his body convulsed as the pain defeated him. Zor averted his eyes.

But suddenly the cadet's fury returned, cutting through the sorrow with a right that started almost at the floor and came up with a loud *crack*! against Zor's chin. Zor fell back against the rec room's bookshelves; he slumped to the floor and looked up at his assailant.

"Feel better now?" Zor asked, wiping blood from his lip.

Eddie's face contorted in rage. He raised his right fist high and stepped in to deliver a follow-up blow, but Angelo Dante had positioned himself in front of Zor.

Eddie's fist glanced off the sergeant's jaw without budging the larger man an inch. Angelo frowned and said, "Don't you think that's enough?"

The cadet was both angry and frightened now. He looked past Angelo, glowering at Zor, and threw the robot head to the floor with all his remaining strength. Then he turned and fled the scene.

Angelo knuckled his bruised cheek. Behind him, Zor said, "Thanks."

"I won't stop him again, Zor," the sergeant said without turning around.

"I don't blame you," Zor returned, full of self-reproach. "I suppose I deserve a lot more than a few punches for what happened to his brother."

Dante didn't bother to argue the fact.

"You got that right, mister," he sneered, walking off.

Zor rode the elevator down to the compound's workout room; it was deserted, as he'd hoped it would be. He took a seat against the room's mirrored wall, regarding the many exercise machines and weight benches in bewilderment, then turned to glance at his reflection.

He had no memory of Eddie Jordon's brother, or of any of the evil deeds the team seemed to hold him responsible for. And without those memories he felt victimized, as much by his own mind as by the teams' often unvoiced accusations. Worse still, the more he did remember, the more correct those accusations appeared. Without exception his dreams and incomplete memory flashbacks were filled with violence and an undefinable but pervasive evil. *It must be true,* he decided. *I have killed other Human beings. . . . I'm a killer,* he told himself—*a killer!*

Zor pressed his hands to his face, his heart filled with remorse for wrongdoings as yet unrevealed. And how *different* this felt than the angry mood he had found himself in earlier the same day!

While he was on the way to the barracks from Nova's post, on the Hovercycle she had requisitioned for his use, Dana had ridden up alongside him, full of her usual optimism and what seemed to be *affection.*

"Have you remembered anything else?" she had asked him.

He practically ignored her.

"Why am I getting the silent treatment all of a sudden?" she had shouted from her cycle. "You've lost your recent memory, too? You've lost all respect for me?"

It was as though something inside him was *forcing* anger against her, irrational but impossible to redirect.

He had snarled at her. "I can't stand the constant interrogation, *Lieutenant.* . . ."

"So! There you are!" he suddenly heard from across the workout room. Dana was standing by the door, impatient with him. "I thought you were going to wait for me in the ready-room. I've been looking all over this place for you."

Zor squeezed his eyes shut, feeling the anger begin to rise in him again, dispersing the sorrow of only moments ago.

"I'm tired of this," he told her, trying his best not to betray the rising tide. "Please leave me alone, Dana."

Dana reacted as though slapped.

"I don't want you bothering me anymore." Something forced the words from his tongue. "And I don't want my memory back either, *understand*?"

"I don't believe what I'm hearing," she said, standing over him now.

Zor stood up and whirled on her. "I can't take this whole situation! If your people want what's locked up in my brain, tell them to *operate*!"

Dana's face clouded over. "You're really hurting me," she said softly. "I'm only trying to help you. I want us to keep being friends. Please ... let me." When he didn't respond she risked a step toward him. "Listen to me, Zor. The past is the past. I don't care what you did. I only know you as you are now. And I think one part of you feels as close to me as I feel to you." She placed her hands on his shoulders and tried to hold his gaze. "Don't run away from this—we can win!"

"No!" he said, turning away from her. "It's over."

She took her hands off him and looked down at the floor. "Okay. If that's the way you want it, then that's it." Then her chin came up. "But don't come looking for me when you need help!"

Dana pivoted through a 180-degree turn and started off, her nose in the air. The room felt unfocused, and it was almost as if she didn't notice the large projection screen that had been positioned against the mirrored wall. Her foot slammed hard into one of the metal frame's support legs and she cursed loudly. But that wasn't enough for her. "You stupid thing!" she barked, and toe-kicked the tubular leg, knocking it free of the frame's weighted foot. The frame began to topple backwards, thick lucite screen and all, and everything seemed to hit the mirrors at the same time.

Instinctively, Zor had rushed forward, aiming to tackle her to safety; but two steps forward he caught sight of himself, reflected in each of the hundreds of mirror shards loosed from the fractured wall.

Past and present seemed to coalesce in that moment: Dana's frightened face became a dark silhouette, then transmutated into the visage of someone ancient and unmistakably evil.

Zzoorrr ... a disembodied voice called to him. *There is*

no place to run. You cannot escape us, you cannot get away. . . .

Now a hand as aged as that face pointed and closed on him open-palmed, and suddenly he found himself running through the curved-top tunnels of some twilight world, fleeing the grasp of armed guardians, caped, helmeted, and curiously armored. A trio of threatening voices pursued him through that labyrinth as well, but ultimately he outran them, launching himself through a hexagonal portal and secreting himself in a darkened room, filled with a heavenly music. . . .

A green-haired woman sat at a harp, her slender fingers forming chords of light that danced about the room. He knew but could not speak her name. Likewise he knew that he had violated a tabu by visiting this place *. . . those ancient ones who sought to control him, to keep him locked away and insulated; those ancient ones who sought to have him absorb a life* he had not lived!

Musica, the green-haired harpist told him. . . .

But he had already moved behind her now, his arm across her neck. The Terminators had caught up with him, and he meant to use her as a shield, a *shield*. . . . *They will not kill her* he told himself, as she quaked with fear in his arms. *She is one of them.*

But the Terminators had armed their weapons and were taking aim; and although he had pushed her aside and fled once more, they had fired—*fired at her*. . . .

The world was blood-red. Someone was calling his name. . . .

Dana was struggling beneath him; he had collapsed over her, shielding her from the glass but pinning her to the floor.

"Musica . . ." Zor heard himself tell her, as she helped him get up. "When I first saw her, she was playing this beautiful music. Then I used her as a shield. . . . I didn't think they'd kill her, but they did!"

Dana was staring at him, her eyes wide. "No, Zor,

they didn't," she tried to tell him. "Bowie *saw* her—*alive*! It must have been a dream—"

Zor was up and walking away from her, fixed on his angry reflection in the shattered mirror.

"I have no memory," he declared, his azure eyes narrowed. "I'm an android. I did kill Eddie's brother, I'm certain of it."

He rammed his right fist into the mirror; then his left, tossing off Dana when she tried to restrain him. Again and again right and left, he punched and whaled at the broken glass, ultimately exhausting himself and reducing his hands to a bloody pulp.

"My god!" he howled. "The Robotech Masters! They must control me completely!"

Dana was leaning against his back, her hands over his shoulders, sobbing.

Zor's nostrils flared. "There's only one way to defeat them—I must destroy myself!"

"No," Dana pleaded with him. "There's always hope. . . ." She caught sight of the fresh blood dripping down the mirror and reached out for his hands. "Your hands!" she gasped. She pulled her kerchief out and wrapped it around his right, which appeared far more lacerated then the left. "Androids don't bleed," she said to him between sobs. "You're Human, Zor—"

"Without a memory? Without a will of my own?"

She wanted to say something, but no words came to her.

"I'm sorry, Dana," Zor told her after a moment. "I've said some terrible things to you. . . ."

"Let me help you," she said, looking into his eyes.

Zor pressed his forehead to hers.

Later, Zor marched determinedly down the halls of the Ministry, closing fast on the office of Rolf Emerson. Dana's help would be invaluable, but there were things he was going to have to do alone. To start with, he needed every scrap of information that was available on the Masters, on their fortresses and science of bio-genetic engineering, and Emerson was the only one who would have access to this.

At the office doors, he stopped and tried to compose himself; then lifted his bandaged hand to knock. He could hear voices coming from the other side of the door.

But something arrested his motion: answering the call of an unknown force, he stood silent and motionless at the threshold, eyes and ears attuned to a kind of recording frequency.

"But it's reckless for Leonard to press an attack now, General," Zor heard Rochelle say. "We aren't prepared."

Rolf Emerson said: "I know, but what can I do? Leonard has most of the staff on his side. I'd hoped this wouldn't happen. I'd hoped to use Zor as a bargaining agent. . . . But instead, it's come down to all-out war."

For several minutes Zor listened at the door, while Emerson and Rochelle summarized the general staff's hastily coordinated attack plans. Then he turned away and walked stiffly down the corridor, his original motivations erased.

Unobserved at the far end of the corridor, Angelo Dante watched Zor leave; tight-lipped, the sergeant nodded his head in knowing confirmation.

The neuro-sensor implanted in Zor's brain now transmitted a steady supply of visual and auditory information, filling the flagship holo-sphere with new images that both troubled and enlightened the three Masters.

"Notice how the clone's rage interferes with our attempts to manipulate his behavior," Bowkaz pointed out, commenting on Zor's blood match with his own reflection. "This is worrisome."

"But even so," Shaizan countered, "the use of the clone goes well—even better than we had hoped." Emerson and Rochelle's exchange of attack plan data underscored the solitary image of a chevroned doorway. "It is interesting, though ... the Micronians continue to delude themselves with plans of attacking our Robotech fortresses."

"I must say they have courage," said Dag.

Shaizan squinted at the holo-sphere's lingering transignal.

"One simple truth remains for the Micronians: we will annihilate every one of them. Annihilate them."

"Annihilate them," Bowkaz repeated.

"Annihilate them!"

CHAPTER
SIXTEEN

"AJACs, my butt! They're nothing but goddamned Proto-copters!"

Remark attributed to an unknown TASC pilot

THE UNITED EARTH GOVERNMENT FLAG FLEW HIGH over the copper-domed Neo-Post-Federalist Senate Building. Inside, Supreme Commander Leonard addressed a combined audience of UEG personnel, Southern Cross officers (Dana Sterling and Marie Crystal among them), representatives of the press, and privileged civilians, from the podium of the structure's vast senatorial hall. Behind him on the stage sat General Rolf Emerson, Colonels Rochelle and Rudolf, and the Joint Chiefs-of-Staff.

"We fully realize there has been much debate over the advisability of a preemptive strike against the alien fleet at this juncture. These concerns have been taken into careful consideration by the High Command of the Armed Forces. But the time has come to put an end to debate, and to unite all our voices behind a common effort.

"Proto-engineering has completed the first consignment of the new Armored Jet Attack Copters, henceforth designated as AJACs. These will form the nucleus of the first assault wave. Your corps commanders will have your individual battle assignments.

"I know there isn't a single soldier in this hall today who isn't painfully aware of all the hazards that will certainly arise during the course of this mission, and there are still some who would advise against its undertaking. But the High Command has determined that we now have the capability of dealing a devastating blow to the enemy, and to do nothing in the face of this advantage is to admit defeat!"

Leonard's speech received less than enthusiastic support, except from certain members of the general staff and the militaristic wing of Chairman Moran's teetering legislature.

Emerson and Rochelle scarcely applauded. Leonard, the two had decided, was a megalomaniac; and the attack plan itself, utter madness.

Afterwards, in front of the building, where the press was all but assaulting Leonard's silver chariot limo, Marie Crystal maneuvered through the crowds to bring her Hovercycle alongside Dana's, just as the 15th's lieutenant was engaging her own mecha's thruster's. Though it was the first time the women had seen each other in several weeks, the reunion was hardly a happy one.

"Guess who's been assigned to the first wave?" Marie taunted her sometime rival. Recently given a clean bill-of-health by the med center staff, she had been reassigned to active duty and reunited with her tactical air squadron.

"Well aren't you the lucky little hotshot, Marie," Dana returned in her sarcastic best. "You're through licking your wounds, huh?" Dana never had paid her that visit— not after what Sean had reported of Marie's continuing quest for a scapegoat.

Marie's cat's-eyes flashed. "Believe me, I'm completely recovered," she told Dana, with a sly grin. "I never felt better in my entire life. But I think it's just *awful* that the Hovertanks won't be seeing any action this time around. Guess you'll be able to get some *training* done while we're gone—heaven knows you need it."

Dana let the remark roll off her back. "To be perfectly honest, I'm really not too unhappy about being grounded," she said in an off-hand manner. "You pilots'll have your hands full."

Marie sniggered. "It won't be that bad. At least this time we'll have a commander who knows what she's doing. Know what I mean?"

Dana frowned, in spite of her best efforts not to. "Oh, why don't you lose that line?" she snapped at Marie. "When are you going to realize that it wasn't my fault?"

Marie laughed, proud of herself. "Don't worry, I forgive you," she said, twisting the throttle and joining the exiting throngs. "So long," she called over her shoulder.

Dana was tempted to send some obscene gesture her way, but thought better of it and reached down to reactivate the thrusters. No sooner had she armed the switch than Nova Satori wandered over.

"Make it brief, Nova," Dana began. "I have to meet Zor in fifteen minutes and he always starts worrying if I'm late."

Nova never had a chance to confront her face-to-face on the medical center stunt, and Dana was in no mood for an argument now. It had been settled officially, and she was willing to let it rest. Although Nova probably didn't see it that way.

"Zor's the very person I wanted to speak to you about."

"Well?" Dana said defensively.

"The GMP appreciates all you've done to help him regain his memory, but we feel there are some areas that only trained professionals can—"

"No!" Dana cut her off. "He's mine and I've promised to help him. These *professionals* you're so proud of will probably make a vegetable of him, and I'm not about to let that happen!"

"Yes, I understand your feelings, Dana," Nova went on in her even voice, "but this case requires some indepth probing of the subject's unconscious mind." Nova glanced at her clipboard, as if reading from a prepared statement. "We've called a certain Dr. Zeitgeist, an expert in alien personality transference to—"

Dana put her hands over her ears. "Enough! You're giving me a monster migraine with all this psychobabble!"

Nova shrugged. "I'm afraid it's out of your hands, Dana. *I've* been assigned to supervise Zor's rehabilitation—"

"Over my dead body, Nova! All he needs is a little Human understanding—something you're in short supply of. Leave him alone!" Dana said, wristing the throttle, hovering off, and almost colliding with an on-coming mega-truck.

"Dana!" the GMP lieutenant called after her. *She's completely lost her objectivity,* Nova said to herself.

"I could just scream sometimes!" Dana said, bursting into the 15th's ready-room.

Cups of coffee and tea slipped from startled hands, chess pieces hit the floor, and permaplas window panes rattled on the other side of the room.

"What seems to be the problem, Lieutenant?" Angelo said, leaping to his feet.

"Nothing!" she roared. "Just tell me where Zor's hiding himself!" Dana's angry strides delivered her over to Bowie. "I thought I told you to keep an eye on him!"

Bowie flinched, stammering a puzzled reply and leaning back not a moment too soon, as Dana's fist came crashing down on the table in front of him. "I can't depend on you for anything at all!"

"Cool your thrusters, Lieutenant," Sean said calmly

from the couch. "The patient's fine and we're keeping tabs on him, so simmer down."

"Well, where is he, Sean?" Dana said quietly but with a nasty edge to her voice.

Sean simply said: "He'll be back in a second," bringing Dana's back up once again.

"I didn't ask you for a timetable of his comings and goings, Private," she barked, hands on her hips. "I want to see him!"

"I think he'd rather you waited. . . ." Sean suggested, as she made to leave the room.

The ready-room doors hissed open. "Just tell me where he is."

"Men's room: straight down the hall, first door on the right."

Dana made a sound of exasperation, while everyone else stifled laughs.

"Any word on assignments from the war council?" Corporal Louie said, hoping to change the subject.

Angelo folded his arms across his chest. "Yeah, do we finally get permission to take care of the enemy this time or do we get held back again?"

Dana walked into their midst. "Well, if you really must know, the Supreme Command in all its infinite wisdom has decided to . . ." she let them hang on her words, ". . . keep us in reserve, of course."

Dana kicked Sean's legs out from under him as she paced past him, forcing him into an involuntary slouch before she exited the ready-room.

"This is getting kinda monotonous," Sean said with a grunt.

Angelo slammed his hands together. "Typical! Whoever makes these stupid decisions oughta be shot!"

Sean extended his legs, crossing his ankles on the table. "It's a crazy idea anyway. I'm telling you, the supreme commander's going nuts. He knows it's hopeless to try a frontal assault."

"The application of brute force is strategically wrong," Louie added, opposite Sean at the table. "We must fight with our intellect . . . By *developing* Robotechnology we stand a chance."

Time would prove him right, but just now Angelo Dante wasn't buying any of it.

"Forget all this machinery!" he counseled. "If they'd just give us a crack at 'em, we'd knock 'em outta the sky!"

Dana went up to her private quarters in the loft above the ready-room, the recent encounters with Marie and Nova replaying themselves in her memory; but these were the reworked and edited versions, now scripted with the things she should have said. She had convinced herself that Nova's spiel was nothing more than a transparent attempt to keep Zor all to herself. And that Marie would undoubtedly try to get her greedy little hands on him, too, once they met—which Dana planned to keep from happening.

She crossed the room and opened the wings of the three-paneled mirror above her vanity, regarding herself with as much objectivity as the moment allowed, sucking in her waist, patting her tummy, and striking fashion poses. She was pleased with her reflection, and decided that there was really nothing to be worried about. Nova didn't stand a chance of keeping Zor to herself. There was simply *no* comparison between Nova's cool prettiness and Dana's warm-blooded allure.

Zor had returned to the ready-room. Angelo was lecturing the others on what he planned to do once he got his hands on the enemy aliens, undisturbed by Zor's presence, actually *playing* to him at times. Zor took a seat across the room and tried to busy himself with a magazine, but his eyes refused to focus on the print; instead they seemed to *demand* that he concentrate his attention on the sergeant. . . .

But Dana's call broke the spell. "Zor, come up here!" she yelled from her quarters. He left the ready-room with the team's laughter at his back and climbed the stairs to the loft.

Dana was standing in front of her vanity when he entered, but what captured his eyes were the three *separate* reflections in the mirror above. Here was Dana in a red dress, Dana in a green pants suit, and Dana in an elegant old-fashioned gown. And yet the *real* Dana was in uniform!

Zor gasped and stumbled, feeling himself drawn once more to the edge of total recall—a dangerous precipice towering out of an absolute darkness.

"Dana...the mirror," he croaked, catching her by surprise. "That...*Triumvirate!*" He didn't know where the word had come from and was at a loss to explain it when she turned her puzzled face to him. "For a moment there were three different images of you in that mirror," he told her anxiously.

She made a wry face. "If you're going to start seeing things, maybe Nova's right and you do need professional help—"

"The Triumvirate!" he interrupted her. "It's starting to come back to me again...."

A chamber filled with a swirling nebulous mixture of liquids and gases, a shape taking form amidst it all—gigantic, inhuman, devoid of all that life was meant to be ... And now a triad of such chambers, but smaller, Human-sized, and within each, beings who shared a common face...

"The Triumvirate...." he groaned, almost losing his balance. "Something to do with acting in groups of three."

Dana seemed almost disinterested in his distress; but in fact, she was beside herself with excitement. Zor had to be making reference to the same triplicate clones she, Bowie, and Louie had seen in the fortress. She was determined to keep Zor unaware of this; and just as determined to prove to Nova that she could handle the subject's unconscious as well as any Dr. Zeitgeist could. From now on it was going to be the kid glove treatment for Zor.

"Well, I have no idea what all that means," she said with elaborate innocence. "But it sounds just screwy enough to turn out to be important. I guess I'll let High Command know about it—even though they're going to think we're *both* crazy," she hastened to add.

At Fokker Field, Lieutenant Marie Crystal, already suited up in gladiatorial, tactical air combat armor, directed her TASC team to one of the score of massive battlecruisers that were positioned about the field in launch mode. Marie checked off names on the list she carried in her mind, as the flyboys rushed by her. Elevators carried them down to the field itself, where Hovertransports were waiting to ferry them to their destinations. In the distance, men and mecha were transferring themselves from transports to cruisers.

Over the PA the voice of a controller issued last minute instructions: *"Final loading of AJACs in assembly bay nineteen. Transport commanders, signal when AJACs are in place. . . . T minus ten minutes to attack launch . . . All pilots to standby alert. . . ."*

Marie checked her suit chronometer against the controller's mark and began to hurry her team along. "Come on," she told them, with a broad sweep of her arm. "Keep it moving! They're not going to wait for us!"

She leaned over the balcony railing to glance at the transports and happened to notice Captain Nordoff's Hoverjeep below. He looked up, spying her and waving his hand.

"We expect to see those AJACs put through their paces up there!" he yelled.

Marie threw him an okay-sign and told him not to

worry about a thing. "I only hope we don't get lost in the shuffle up there—I've never seen so many ships!"

"Just pray we've got enough, Lieutenant!" he said, and hovered off.

Marie straightened up from the rail and turned to find Sean alongside her, displaying his well-known roguish grin.

"Hello, *Private*," Marie said disdainfully.

"Hey, don't get personal," Sean laughed.

She turned her back to him. "What are you doing here, Sean? No hot date today? After all, the Fifteenth's not part of this action."

"Hey, don't say things like that, Marie," he said peevishly. "You're tearing me apart, you know that? I came here because I wanted to see you off. I care about you, in case you haven't guessed."

Marie looked at him over her shoulder. "Don't think that one night on the roof makes us an item, Sean," she warned him. "I trust you just about as far as I can throw you."

"T minus six minutes to launch," the controller told them from the tower. *"All commanders to their posts...."*

Neither one of them said anything for a moment; then Sean broke the silence with a quiet. "Be careful, okay?"

Marie's hard look softened. "I almost believe you really mean that...."

"I, I mean it," he stammered.

Marie blew him a kiss from the elevator.

Elsewhere on the base, Zor stood alone, his azure eyes scanning the field, an unwitting transmitter of sight and sound....

In the Robotech flagship, the three Masters watched over the Earth Forces base through the clone's eyes. The Protoculture cap was beneath their aged hands now as they readied their fleet for battle.

"This new armada is the single largest fleet they have

yet dared to send against us," Bowkaz saw fit to point out, no suggestion of fear or anticipation in his deep voice.

"The more ships they employ, the greater our triumph," said Dag.

"Their armada will be destroyed and their spirit broken," Shaizan added. But suddenly there were signs of interrupted concentration in the transignal holo-image. "What is happening?" he asked the others.

Bowkaz repositioned his hands on the Protoculture cap, but the image of the prelaunch battlecruisers continued to waver and ultimately de-rezzed entirely. "Someone is interfering with the clone," he explained. "Distracting him. . . ."

While Dana had excused herself to notify Rolf Emerson of Zor's latest flashback, the alien himself had left the barracks. All at once compelled to visit the Earth Forces launch site, he had ridden his Hovercycle up to the plateau, and chosen a spot near the field that offered a vantage point for all the myriad activities taking place. In a certain sense he was not cognizant of where he was, nor what he was doing; and equally unaware that both Angelo and Dana, on separate cycles, had followed him there.

The sergeant had watched Zor for some time, wondering what his next move might be; but when he realized that the alien was simply staring transfixed at the prelaunch activities, he decided to move in.

"Just what the hell do you think you're doing up here, Zor?" he demanded, seemingly awakening Zor from a dream. "This sector's off-limits. And besides, you're supposed to be back at the barracks."

"I was trying to get a better view of the liftoff," Zor offered as explanation, although one part of him realized this wasn't true.

Angelo took a quick glance right and left; there was no

one in sight, and Angelo was tempted to fix it so the alien
would no longer be *capable* of moving around scot-free.
Dante took a menacing step forward, only to hear Dana's
voice behind him.

"It's all right, Sergeant, I'll vouch for him."

Angelo glared at Zor and relaxed some. Dana was
marching up the small rise to join them, breathless when
she arrived. She glanced briefly at Zor, then threw the
sergeant a suspicious look.

"What did you have in mind, Angelo?" she asked him,
her chin up.

Dante met her gaze and said: "Not a thing, Lieutenant."

Dana nodded warily. "I gave Zor clearance to go wherever he wants. I thought it might help him get his memory
back."

"Or something," said Angelo.

Zor looked at both of them, beginning to feel the
anger return.

Supreme Commander Leonard and his staff viewed
the armada liftoff from command central's underground
bunker. The darkly armored leviathanlike battlecruisers
were underway, rising from the plateau base like a school
of surfacing whales.

"Just look at them!" Leonard gushed, his eyes glued to
the monitor screen. "How can they possibly fail?"

"Very impressive, Commander," said Rolf Emerson,
giving lip-service to the moment. *I wish to heaven I shared
your confidence,* he kept to himself.

Schematics of the attack force and the relative position
of the Masters' fleet were carried to the oval screen in the
flagship command center.

"Ah, here they come," said Bowkaz. "Like the prover-
bial moths to the flame."

"Is there no one among them who sees the stupidity of this?" Dag asked rhetorically.

"I will summon our defense force," said Shajzan.

But Bowkaz told him not to bother. "This won't require the rest of the fleet. One ship will be sufficient."

■ ■ ■ ■ ■ ■ ■ ■ ■ ■ ■ ■ ■ ■ ■ ■

CHAPTER
SEVENTEEN

With Dana Sterling's penetration of the SDF-1 burial mound, Humankind [on Earth] had observed three separate stages of the Optera lifeform and still didn't recognize what they were seeing: Lynn-Minmei had watched Khyron ingesting the dried leaves, Sean Phillips had actually tossed the fruit of the tree in his hand, and Dana Sterling had seen the plants in full flower. All this intrigue centered on Protoculture, when the real treasure was in front of them all the time—the Flower of Life itself!...Only one stage remained, but Humankind would have to await the Invid's arrival to glimpse it. In thinking about it, though, one might almost say that the Invid were the final stage!

Maria Bartley-Rand, *Flower of Life: Journey Beyond Protoculture*

GENERAL LEONARD'S ATTACK PLAN WAS A BASIC one ("simple-minded," as Rolf Emerson would call it later): meet the enemy's six spade fortresses head-on with the more than fifty battlecruisers of the Earth Forces armada; use the new AJAC gunships to confuse them; then, simply overwhelm them with superior firepower. Captain Nordoff would supervise the first-wave assault; Admirals Clark and Salaam would take it from there. There were no tactics built into the plan, no flanking or diversionary operations, no contingencies for possible setbacks. The attack, which Leonard had optimistically (and unrealistically) labeled *preemptive*, would render needless Angelo Dante's concerns that Zor might be an enemy agent; the Robotech Masters hardly needed the clone's eyes to see what was coming, and consequently they were more than prepared.

At a distance of 100 miles from the alien fortresses (which were still holding in geosynchronous orbit, some 47,000 miles above the Equator), Nordoff gave the order to open fire. Annihilation discs streamed from the cruiser's pulsed laser cannon like so many small golden suns—energy-Frisbees that to the last found their targets. But the enemy defense shields absorbed it all and gave every indication of being hungry for more. The great horned and spiked fortresses were not only left undamaged, but *untouched* as well.

Knowing how much was riding on the success of the first wave, Nordoff ordered his wing to maintain course and continue firing, even if that meant at point-blank range. An armchair tactician, Nordoff, not unlike Commander Leonard, refused to accept the fact that the fortresses were effectively invincible—this despite the projections and cautions of the Southern Cross's most brilliant minds. Even the 15th Squadron's downing of the alien flagship was now being reevaluated in terms of the Masters's own allowances and strategies.

At less than sixty-five miles the first-wave battlecruisers launched a second fusillade; but this time the annihilation discs were not absorbed: they were added to the fortresses' already immeasurably charged stockpiles and spit back. Radiant blue-white tentacles reached out from the lead fortress and grappled with one of the battlecruisers, probing indelicately for weak spots in its armored hull. Troops were caught unawares by the force, incinerated in a thousand flashstorms that swept through the ship, or sent spinning to vacuum death through ruptures which instantaneously bled precious atmosphere from the already scorched and scoured holds.

In the AJACs launch bay aboard Nordoff's ship, Marie Crystal heard that what remained of the 007 was dead in space. She had been supervising the launch preparations for the choppers, but now ran from her post to one of the starboard cannon turrets, literally kicking the gunner from his seat to have a crack at the enemy herself. She had good friends aboard the demolished cruiser and wasn't about to allow their deaths go unpunished.

Once in the turret seat, Marie quickly removed her helmet and strapped on the weapon's sensor-studded targeting cap. As computer-generated graphic displays flashed across the helmet's virtual cockpit, she immediately realized why the first-wave had failed to cripple the enemy flagship: Nordoff and the other commanders were completely disregarding intel analysis reports concerning the fortresses' vulnerable spots. Concentrated fire directed at any one of these would circumvent the shields' absorption potential and allow pulses to penetrate to the hull itself.

Marie had been close enough to these things in the past to have committed their surface details to memory; in fact, during her recent hospitalization (when she wasn't glancing at muscle mags), she had done little else except replay the fortresses' topography over and over to herself. Ranging in the gun now, she felt as though she were directly over the fortress in her Logan and could place the shot precisely where she wanted it.

"Ah-ha! There you are!" she said out loud as the spot was centered in the cannon's reticle. Marie pulled home the twin hand-brake-like triggers and loosed a full ten-seconds of plasma fire at the flagship, knowing almost before the fact that she had scored a direct hit.

In the flagship command center, the three Masters hardly reacted to news that one of the fortress barriers had been breached. Absorbing the energy discs delivered by the Terrans' cruisers had enabled them to leave their own plasma reservoirs untouched and therefore shunt would-be weapons system power to the fortresses' shields and self-restorative systems.

No sooner had Marie's well-aimed barrage holed the

hull than new plating was already sliding into place to seal the breach.

Dag suggested that it might not even be necessary to fire on the Terrans; better to let them fall back in complete confusion, demoralized by their futile attempt.

But Bowkaz wanted to see concrete results.

The fortress fired back, taking out two more battle-cruisers.

Dana and Zor had left their Hovercycles at the base and set out on foot for the grassy overlook high above Monument City. Dana had sent Dante back to command the 15th in her absence, ignoring his reminders that just because the ground-based tactical armored units weren't directly involved in the battle they were nevertheless still on standby alert. Not that he had expected her to abandon her pet project and return to the barracks; and the only reason the sergeant didn't bother to press his point (or, for that matter, inform Sterling's commanders) was that he felt a lot better off without the alien around—and that went for both Zor *and* Dana.

Dana was encouraged by Zor's most recent mention of "the Triumvirate" to resort to what she considered high-risk therapy now, and as they walked and talked, she was sorely tempted to confess her past to him, certain that he would then move even closer to recovering his own. It was of course a double-edged sword and she was aware of the ambivalence within her: on the one hand, Zor's memory could turn out to be the key that would unlock the mystery of the Robotech Masters and give Earth the data it needed to mount a proper defense, or, as Rolf hoped, engage in some sort of deal-making. But on the other, Dana liked having this past-less Zor by her side, this empty mind she could fill with the memories she wanted placed there; in a way there was something nurturing and maternal about the whole thing that went side-by-side with the more primitive feelings she had for Zor.

They had reached the flat grassy area now, lifeless crags and shale rivers ascending on three sides, with the last open to a spectacular view of the city, several thousand yards below them. Dana tried not to think about George Sullivan and the few moments the two of them had shared here.

The sky was not cloudless, but deeply sky-blue nonetheless, and the air was unusually warm, especially for this altitude.

Zor must have been aware of it, too, because he commented that it was hard to believe there was a war going on.

"It's so peaceful and quiet up here," she told him as they walked. "I always start thinking about where I grew up when I come up here . . . the people I left behind."

It would have been better to tell him about where her *mother* grew up, she added silently. That would undoubtedly interest him a lot more than stories about Rolf's farm and the almost idyllic childhood she and Bowie had shared—until military school, that was, and Rolf's appointment to general and their move from New Denver to Monument City.

But Zor didn't ask for any specifics about that place; instead, he asked with a laugh: "Was one of the people you left behind a boyfriend?"

It sounded so ridiculous coming from him that for a moment she was certain he was joking with her. So she played cryptic to his question and said, "No, not really . . ."

They were overlooking the city now, and Zor sat down in the tall grass to take in the view. "I wish I could remember where I grew up," he said wistfully. "I guess I'll never know what it's like to go home again."

"Well, the war will be over someday," she suggested. "You could think about starting a new home . . ."

Zor had pulled up a long blade of grass and was chewing at one end of it absently. "No," he told her. "It's not as simple as that. A man without a past is a man without a home—now and always."

"But each day brings a little more of your past back to you," she reminded him encouragingly.

"That's true," he admitted haltingly. "I do remember something about the Triumvirate and Musica...but mainly it's these terrible visions about death and destruction. I know I was doing something important when the enemy attacked. And I get this feeling that there were *giants* there to protect me...but after that, all I can think about is bloodshed, devastation." Zor pressed the heels of his hands to his temples. "If only I could remember where and why that attack took place. But there's nothing there. Just a blank."

"Don't put yourself through it now, Zor."

"And those strange mounds that Nova showed me before I passed out..."

"Mounds?" Dana said all of a sudden. "You didn't tell me about this!"

"That's when we weren't speaking. When I was staying at the GMP headquarters."

"Of course! Why haven't I thought of this before?!"

Suddenly Dana had a flash of insight: the mounds, of course! Zor had been there. There was no reason to think that the mounds would do it for him after Bowie hadn't, but it was worth a chance.

Dana stood up, took hold of Zor's hand, and led him off in a run.

Nearby, a curious animal poked its head from the tall grass. From a distance it might have been mistaken for a small shaggy dog; but up close several differences immediately presented themselves: the two knob-ended horns that rose from behind its sheepdog forelock, the feet like soft muffins, the eyes that were not of this Earth.

There was something about the creature's pose and expression that suggested disbelief. It recognized its one-time female friend. But it was the other human that captivated the creature's attention just now: it was the being who had taken it from its homeworld.

The creature had almost run to this one, caught up in an instinctual desire to be taken home. But instead, it followed the two Humans from a discreet distance.

Nordoff had had a change of mind.

"A third of our battle fleet and nearly half our transports have already been lost," he reported to the war room. "They're tearing us to shreds! Sir, it's impossible for us to maintain battle formation. I suggest we withdraw immediately."

"Nonsense," said Leonard into the remote mike. "Why haven't you brought the AJACs to bear against the enemy, Captain?"

"We've been awfully busy just trying to *survive* up to this point," Nordoff returned. "Sir," he continued with greater emphasis, "the enemy has been dispatching our largest battlecruisers with regularity; I hardly think attack choppers have a—"

"Captain, this is a question for me to decide. Follow your instructions. Dispatch the AJACs!"

Dana felt Bowie's presence essential; so she and the alien returned to the 15th's barracks and snatched Bowie from the ready-room before setting off for the place where Zor and Dana had first set eyes on each other, and where Bowie himself had been held captive—the burial site of the SDF-1.

Once again Angelo Dante didn't bother to protest, happy to be rid of the three of them, liabilities all. Now the sergeant said to himself, if he could only do something about Sean and a few of the others. But when he completed his mental list of rejects he found that he had eliminated all but one man from the 15th—*himself*!

Meanwhile, the therapist, her assistant, and their patient powered their Hovercycles to the top of the ridge and over the pass that linked Monument with what was once its sister city, Macross. There was no actual roadway left, but there were remnants of the original one, and the cycles easily allowed them to scramble around rough spots and landslide areas—both natural and deliberate.

Macross was theoretically off-limits to civilians and Southern Cross troops alike, although the site was in no way patrolled or otherwise kept under surveillance. It was a well-known fact that the final battle between the SDFs 1 and 2 and the Zentraedi warship manned by Khyron and his consort, Azonia, had left the area intensely radio-active. Whether this was still the case was top-secret and a question that could only be answered by Professor Zand or one of those few scientists who had served on the dimensional fortress and had not for one reason or another elected to accompany Lang, Hunter, and Edwards on the Expeditionary Mission to Tirol. In any case, the High Command didn't want anyone poking around: most of the usable mecha and Robotechnological marvels had been salvaged from the ship, but Lang had given strict orders that no one was to disturb the area. Hence, the two-fold purpose of the bulldozed mounds themselves.

The lakebed had dried up and the resultant bowl was now teeming with a wide assortment of vegetal and animal life, reminiscent of some of the atypical habitats that formed in the bottom of craters or calderas, like that of Ngorongoro in East Africa. And in the center of this were the three flat-topped mounds, steep-sided, with larger bases than crowns, capped with vegetation, and shrouded in mystery.

Dana brought the trio to a halt some distance from the mounds. She turned to glance at Zor, looking for any signs that might indicate familiarity or recall. But instead, Zor seemed puzzled and possibly spooked, as she herself felt.

"Well you know that 'military base' you keep dreaming about—the one that was attacked?" Dana began. "It occurred to me that this might be it. Bowie and I *saw* you here, Zor—we *fought* against you and your Bioroids *right on this spot!*" Dana looked apologetic. "I didn't want to tell you before, because Nova insists that I'm not to *plant* memories in your mind . . . but this place is so important. You actually held Bowie prisoner here, Zor. Don't you remember any of it?"

Zor was looking at Bowie for confirmation and receiving it; but even that had no apparent effect. Zor tightened his mouth and shook his head.

"There was a terrible battle fought here," Bowie added. "Between the Earth Forces and the last of the Zentraedi—a race sent here by your Masters to retrieve something they thought we had—something they believe we *still* have." Bowie gestured to the three mounds. "Underneath one of these are the remains of a ship that was probably sent to Earth from your homeworld, a planet called Tirol. By someone who you might even be related to—a being called Zor."

Zor listened without a word, as an animal might listen to Human speech: aware of the tone and even the words, but ignorant of the sense of it.

"My father's sister, my aunt, died here," Bowie said softly, his voice cracking. "Her name was Claudia Grant."

"I'm sorry for that," Zor returned. "And what was this thing you were supposed to have that my Masters are still so desperate for?" he asked them.

Dana spoke to this, shrugging first, to indicate her limited knowledge of these things. "Some kind of generator. Something that has to do with Protoculture—the sort of *fuel* that drives our mecha and permits our Veritechs to transform."

"To reconfigure," Zor said, at the edge of something. He absently gnawed at his lower lip. "Protoculture . . ." he said thoughtfully. "I don't know . . . It does seem familiar; but I don't recall anything."

"Well since we're here, let's poke around some," Dana

proposed. "Maybe we'll find something to jog your memory. I mean, if you feel up to it . . ." she thought to add.

"Of course I am," Zor assured her, straightening himself in the cycle's seat. "I'll investigate the mound on the left."

"I'll take the right one," Bowie said eagerly.

Dana smiled and worked the mecha's throttle. "Okay. Then let's get cracking!"

Zor and Bowie hovered off and she did the same, heading for the center mound, which up close proved to be somewhat larger than the others. But like them, it had the same atmosphere of enchantment and eerieness lingering about it, the same profusion of shrubs, saplings, and underbrush growing from crevices in its steep sides.

Out of sight the pollinator watched her, and began to head toward the same mound.

She saw nothing that might indicate a way into the mound and considered attempting to power her cycle up the sides for a look at the top; but first decided to circle around the thing once or twice to see what she could find. Just shy of completing the circle she found what she was looking for: something like the mouth of a cave, large, dark and fanged by stalactite-like deposits. She called out for Bowie and Zor to join her, and in moments they were by her side.

They dismounted their cycles and made their way up to the mouth of the opening, scrambling over rocks and through the barbed and tenacious growth that covered the mound's inclined lower base. At the mouth, Bowie bravely stepped in, and stood for a moment in the darkness waiting for his eyes to dark-adapt.

"It looks like it goes all the way in," he told Zor and Dana.

They followed. Even Zor seemed to have misgivings. "Let's be careful," he told Dana. "We don't know *what* we might find in here."

"Now, when have I not been careful?" She laughed,

hopping over a rock at the entrance and starting in, passing Bowie by.

It wasn't a natural opening in the side of the mound; it appeared to have been excavated. Dana began to wonder whether looters had worked over the sites during the past fifteen years.

They moved cautiously through the darkness, alert to distant sounds.

"It's like a tomb in here—all this place needs are a few mummies," said Bowie.

"Stop that," Dana told him. "I'm scared enough already."

As they penetrated further, one thing was immediately obvious: although there were indeed organic deposits growing from the ceiling of the cave (some twenty-yards high) and vines and whatnot clinging to the walls, the cave was in no way natural—they were actually inside an enormous corridor. Exposed panels and circuitry, rusting structural members and bulkheads confirmed this much.

But there were live things in the corridor as well, as Dana was soon to find out.

Without warning, a group of bats flew straight at them out of the darkness. Dana screamed, launched, and latched herself onto Zor's arm, instantly regretting her show of weakness.

She reached up to find his mouth in the darkness, angrier when she felt a smile there.

Zor laughed and insisted that they keep going.

They moved along the corridor for another fifteen minutes, following it along a gentle arc; then there was light ahead of them—what appeared to be a free-standing monolithic light bar, but was in fact a narrow opening in the wall of the corridor, permitting light to issue forth from somewhere deeper inside the mound.

Zor volunteered to take the point on this one, feeling as though he was indeed approaching something that would lead him to clues of his real origins and past. He seemed to know this place somehow, the feel of these corridors. It was not quite the same as the picture his mind drew of it, but familiar nevertheless. In a strange way, he felt that he knew this place as one would a home.

The opening was just large enough to slip into, but it required that he keep his shoulders pressed flat against the wall. It had to be a ventilation shaft or accessway that was not meant to be walked.

Dana and Bowie stuck close. "Can you see?" Dana asked Zor. "Are we almost at the end?"

"A little more . . ." he told her.

And all at once they were through the breach and inside an enormous chamber. Below them was what seemed to be an excavated pit. Rough staircases had been cut into the dirt and debris that settled into the place when the roof caved in possibly a decade or more ago. Shafts of sunlight poured in through openings in the crust above, along with vines and the off-shoots of trees.

But the pit itself was what struck them: from a viscous-looking organic soup all but bubbling in the bottom of the cauldron, grew an orderly pattern of strange, unearthly green stalks, blossoming with fragrant buds and tripetaled flowers even as they watched.

Overhead, light, mist, and bioenergy given off by the plants conspired to form what looked to be an arrangement of power coils.

"This place is unbelievable," said Dana. "It's throbbing with power . . . and those plants . . . What on Earth are they?"

"It's like some kind of greenhouse," Bowie suggested.

The trio made their way down the roughly-hewn staircase until they were standing at the very edge of the cauldron. The plants swayed, as though moved by some wind only they could detect. More, they seemed to be communing with each other, issuing a song that circumvented normal Human hearing. Dana felt compelled to reach out toward one of the flowers, just to stroke the velvety surface of its petals...

"No, don't touch that!" Zor yelled.

But it was too late. The flower seemed to meet Dana's hand halfway and attach itself to her. She felt no pain from this, but Zor's yell had startled her so, that she quickly snatched her hand away.

Bowie was aghast. "The plant sensed you, Dana! Did you see it move toward you?"

Zor was now standing transfixed by the scene, mesmerized by the shafts of dazzling light and something that played at the edge of his memory.

"The Triumvirate!..." he said suddenly. "Look at these flowers—they grow in threes!—the *three who act as one*! Once again, the same thing I saw in my dream."

Dana tried to coax more from his tortured mind. "Could those things be related somehow?"

"Do you think maybe these plants are what the Masters are trying to get their hands on?" Bowie asked.

Zor shook his head, eyes shut tight. "I don't know... But I do know that these flowers aren't what they seem. They're some kind of dreadful mutation, feeding off a source of incredible power. They're definitely a new form of life, unlike any that we've ever seen."

Dana turned to regard the cauldron, the writhing plants, their siren song...

"I don't like this at all..." she said warily.

Zor concurred. "Neither do I," he told her. "I feel this cavern is full of emanations of great strength. It's as if these plants were calling out... making contact with something far away. My past is buried here somehow. But how can I expect anyone to believe this?"

"We'll bring the Supreme Commander here and show it to him—he'll have to believe you then!"

"Oh, terrific!" Bowie exclaimed. "Can you imagine what he'd say to that—'You expect me to believe this

balderdash about flowers and strange emanations?'...
That's what he'd say! He'd think we're crazy, Dana."

Dana took a deep breath and reached for Zor's hand.

General Emerson and Colonel Rochelle sat silently in
the war room. The assault had proved to be a total disaster, to men and mecha alike. Dozens of battlecruisers had
been lost, along with an untold number of the AJACs the
supreme command had put so much faith in.

Nova Satori was with the two men; she had volunteered to get some coffee for all of them, and was returning with steaming mugs when ground-base com
acknowledged an incoming message from Lieutenant
Sterling. Emerson had the techs patch the transmission
through to the command balcony, and in a moment
Dana's face filled the monitor screen.

"First of all, sir...I'm fully aware that I disobeyed
orders."

"So, what else is new?" Nova muttered behind the
general's back.

Dana caught the comment and replied to it. "I'm sorry,
Nova, but I have Zor with me and we've just paid a visit
to the site of the SDF-1. General, I hope you're not too
angry with us."

Depleted of emotion, Emerson simply snorted. Besides, he had interesting news of his own to report—perhaps the only good news that had come from the battle.

"Lieutenant," he began. "We've just received a transmission from Marie Crystal. She was in direct contact
with the enemy and her visual evidence seems to bear out
that theory of yours regarding the trichotomous pattern
of the aliens' behavior."

"I can't take credit for it, sir. It was Zor's idea. Is
Marie all right?"

"Our losses were disastrously heavy...But I've been
informed that Lieutenant Crystal is now safely back
aboard. She and the entire first assault wave have disen-

gaged and are withdrawing toward the dark side of the moon. However, I regret to say that the attack has been something of a fiasco."

In another part of the UEG headquarters, Leonard was receiving the most recent battle update.

"Supreme Commander," a tech reported from the monitor, "the first assault wave has fallen back in disarray."

"Well then, we'll demonstrate that we have more where that came from," Leonard growled.

"Sir? . . ."

"Mobilize the second assault wave. Order them to rendezvous with the remaining operational units of the first wave and prepare for a combined attack against the enemy."

The tech went wide-eyed with disbelief. "Another frontal assault, Supreme Commander?"

Leonard ran a thick hand across his bullet-shaped skull and nodded gravely.

"And this time, we'll fight to the very last Human life!"

The following chapter is a sneak preview of THE FINAL NIGHTMARE—Book 9 in the continuing saga of RO-BOTECH!!

CHAPTER
ONE

Many women were often in the thick of the fighting during the First Robotech War. They served splendidly and well, but they were often restricted to what the military insisted on calling "non-combat roles," despite the great numbers of them killed as a direct result of enemy action.

By the time of the Second Robotech War, with the Earth's resources depleted and its population drastically reduced by the First, sheer necessity and common sense had overcome the lingering sexism that had kept willing, qualified women off the front lines.

Nevertheless, the Robotech Masters' onslaught quickly had the Earth on the ropes. It is instructive to consider what the outcome would have been if the Army of the Southern Cross had faced the planet's second invasion without half its fighting strength.

Fortunately for us all, that is not what happened.

Betty Greer, *Post-Feminism and the Robotech Wars*

LIEUTENANT MARIE CRYSTAL MADE A WILLFUL effort to face the camera now as she had faced enemy guns yesterday.

She drove back her bone-deep exhaustion, the pain of battle injuries, and the despair of a desperate situation that even the light lunar gravity couldn't alleviate. She intended to finish her report with the clarity and precision expected of a Tactical Armored Space Corps fighter ace and the leader of the TASC's vaunted Black Lions . . .

And maybe, after that, she could collapse and get a few minutes' sleep. It seemed now that she never wanted anything *but* sleep.

In the wake of the disastrous all-out attempt to destroy the Robotech Masters' invasion fleet, Marie had to shoulder even more responsibility. The chain of command had been shot all to hell along with the Earth strikeforce itself.

Admiral Burke was dead—diced into bloody stew by an exploding power junction housing when the blue Bioroids cut the strikeforce flagship to ribbons. General Lacey, next in line, lay with ninety percent of the skin seared off his body, teetering between life and death.

The senior officer still functional was a staff one-star, but he had virtually no combat command experience. The scuttlebutt was that he was being pressured to let somebody else run the show. An implausibly successful Bioroid sortie and the resultant hangar deck explosion onboard the now-defunct flagship resulted in Marie being named the new Flight Group Commander.

She went on with her after-action report to Southern Cross military headquarters on Earth.

"Our remaining spacecraft number: one battlecruiser, two destroyer escorts, and one logistical support ship, all of which have suffered heavy damage," she said, looking squarely into the optical pickup. "Along with twenty-three Veritech fighters, twelve AJAC combat mecha, and assorted small scout and surveillance ships. At last report we have one thousand, one hundred sixteen surviving personnel, eight hundred and fifty seven of them fit for duty."

Fewer than nine hundred effectives! Jesus! She pulled at the collar ring seal of her combat armor, where it had chafed her neck. She couldn't recall the last time she had been able to strip off the alloy plate and get some real rest. Back on Earth, probably. But that was a lifetime ago.

"As I stated previously, deployment of the enemy mother ships, and their assault craft and Bioroid combat mecha, made it impossible for the strikeforce to return to Earth. Since we were also cut off from L5 space station *Liberty*, and were forced to take refuge here at Moon Base ALUCE, we are making round-the-clock efforts to fortify our position against an enemy counter attack. Major repairs and life-support replenishment are being carried out as well, and civilian personnel have been placed under emergency military authority."

It all sounded so crisp, so can-do, she thought, trying to focus her eyes on her notecards. As if everything were under control, instead of at the thin edge of utter catastrophe. As if the survivors were an effective fighting force instead of a chewed up, burned-out bunch of men and women and machinery. As if the attack hadn't been the most insane strategy, the worst snafu, the most horrifying slaughter she had ever seen.

Recording her stiff-upper-lip report, she felt like a liar, but that was the way Marie Crystal had been taught to do her duty. She wondered if the brass hats at Southern Cross Army HQ back on Earth would read between the lines—if that pompous, blustering idiot, Supreme Commander Leonard, had any idea how much suffering and death he had caused.

She yanked her mind off that track; feeling murderous toward her superiors wouldn't help now.

"Our medical personnel and volunteers from other strikeforce elements are tendng to the wounded in the ALUCE medcenter. But facilities are extremely limited here, and I am instructed to request that we be permitted to attempt a special mission to ferry our worst cases back to Earth."

What could she add? There was the natural Human impulse to tell the goddamn lardbutts in their swivel chairs how much hell she had seen. There was the desire to see someone capable, someone like General Emerson, for instance, march in before the United Earth Government council and charge Leonard and his staff with incompetence. There was an inner compulsion to tell how futile it felt. She was working against impossible odds, preparing the civilian ALUCE—Advanced Lunar Chemical Engineering—station for a last stand, and getting the

VTs and other mecha ready to sortie out again if the need arose.

Forget it; shoot 'n' salute, that was a soldier's duty. Maybe a miracle would happen, and the mysterious aliens who called themselves the Robotech Masters would cut ALUCE and the strikeforce a little slack. If the Humans could just have a few days to get themselves back into some kind of fighting shape, that would change the mix a lot. But Marie had her doubts.

"This completes the situation report. Lieutenant Marie Crystal, reporting for the Commander, out." She saluted smartly, her mouth tugging in a faint, ironic smirk.

The camera tech wrapped it up. "We'll transcribe it and send it out in burst right away, ma'am." She took the cassette of Marie's report.

The Robotech Masters had been having more and more success interfering with the frequency-jumping communications tactics the Humans had been forced to use. To avoid any interference, the report would be sped up to a millisecond squeal of information. Hopefully it would get through.

And when they get it, what then? Marie wondered. *We might be able to sneak one shipload of WIAs back, but for the rest of us there's no way home.*

In the headquarters of the Army of the Southern Cross, Supreme Commander Leonard studied the tape. The smudged and hollow-eyed young female flight lieutenant reeled off facts and figures of bitter defeat with no expression except that last upcurling of one corner of her mouth.

"Mmm," was all he said, as Colonel Rochelle turned off the tape.

"We received this transmission from ALUCE eight minutes ago, sir," Rochelle told him. "Nothing else has gotten through the enemy's jamming so far. Looks like they're onto our freq-jumping stunt. The people down in signal/crypto are trying to come up with something new, but so far the occasional odd message is all we can really hope for from Strikeforce Victory."

Leonard nodded slowly, looking at the huge, gray screen. Then he whirled around and threw himself into a seat across the conference table from Major General Rolf Emerson.

"Well, Emerson! How about that!" Leonard pounded his pale, soft, freckled fists the size of pot roasts on the gleaming oak. "It would appear that our little assault operation wasn't a complete failure after all, eh?"

Everyone in the room held their breath. It was a well-known fact that Emerson had opposed the mad Strikeforce scheme the outset, and that there was no love lost between the Supreme Commander and his chief of staff for Terrestrial Defense, Emerson. And everyone had watched Emerson grow grimmer and grimmer as Marie Crystal delivered her casualty report.

Now Emerson looked across the table at Leonard, and more than one staff officer wished they had had time to get a little money down on the fight. Leonard was huge, but a lot of it was pointless bulk; there was some question about how much real muscle was there. Emerson, on the other hand, was a ramrod-straight middleweight with a boxer's physique, and few of the men and women on his staff could keep up with him when it came time for calisthenics or road drill.

Not a complete failure? Emerson was asking himself. *God, what* would *this man call "failure"?*

But he was a man bound by his oath. A generation before, military officers had violated their oaths. They had served grasping politicians—most tellingly in the now-defunct USA, and that had led to a global civil war. Every woman and man who had sworn to serve the Southern Cross Army knew those stories, and knew that it was their obligation to obey that oath to the letter.

Emerson stared down at his fingers which were curled around an ancient fountain pen that had been a gift from his ward, Private First Class Bowie Grant. He worried about Bowie only slightly more than he worried about each of the hundreds and thousands of other Southern Cross Army personnel under his command. He worried about the survival of the Human race and that of Earth more than he worried about any individual Human life—even his own.

Emerson gathered up all of his patience, and the perserverence for which he was so famous. "Commander Leonard, the ALUCE base is a mere research outpost, with civilians present. Aside from the fact that by the standards of the Robotech war we're fighting, ALUCE is tin foil and cardboard! I therefore presume you're not seriously thinking of fortifying it as a military base."

It was as close to insubordination as Emerson had ever permitted himself to go. The silence in the Command Briefing Room was so profound that the roiling of various stomachs could be heard. Through it all, Emerson was locked with Leonard's gaze.

The Supreme Commander spoke deliberately. "Yes, that is my plan. And I see nothing wrong with it!" He seemed to be making it up as he went along. "Mmm. As I see it, a military strikeforce at an outpost on the moon will enable us to hit those alien bastards from two different directions at once!"

A G3 staff light colonel named Rudolph readjusted his glasses and said eagerly, "I see! In that way, we're outflanking those six big mother ships they've got in orbit around Earth!"

Leonard looked pleased. "Yes. Precisely."

Emerson took a deep breath and pushed his chair away from the oak table a little, as though he was about to face a firing squad. But when he came to his feet, there was silence. All eyes turned to him. The general feeling was that no one on Earth was more trusted, more committed to standing by his word, than Rolf Emerson.

No one could be relied upon more to speak the truth into the teeth of deceit.

And this was certainly that moment. "ALUCE is a peaceful unreinforced cluster of pressurized huts Commander Leonard. I don't think that anything the Strike-force survivors can do will make it a viable military base. And it's my opinion that by provoking the enemy into attacking it you'll be throwing away lives."

So many staffers inhaled at the same time that Rudolph wondered if the air pressure would drop. Leonard's faced flushed with rage. "They've already mauled our first assault wave; it's not a question of provocation anymore. *Damn* it, man! This is war, not an exercise in interstellar diplomacy!"

"But we haven't even *tried* negotiating," Emerson began, a little hopelessly. An over-eager missile battery commander named Komodo had fired on the Robotech Masters before any real attempt could be made to contact them and learn what it was they wanted. From that moment on, it had been war.

"I'll have no insubordination!" Leonard bellowed. To the rest of the staff he added, "Mobilize the second strikeforce and prepare them to relieve our troops at Moon Base ALUCE!"

Outside the classified-conference room, a figure clad in the uniform of the Southern Cross's Alpha Tactical Armored Corps—the ATACs—moved furtively.

Zor still didn't quite understand the half-perceived urges that had brought him there. It was a familiar feeling—this utter mystification about who he was, and what forces drove him. It was as though he moved in a fog, but he knew that somewhere ahead was the room where all Earth's military plans were being formulated. He must go there, he must listen and watch—but he didn't understand why.

Suddenly there was a bigger figure blocking his way. "Okay, Zor. Suppose you tell me just what the hell you think you're doing here?"

It was Sergeant Angelo Dante, senior NCO of the

15th, fists balled and feet set at about shoulder width, ready for a fight. His size and strength dwarfed Zor's—and Zor was not small. Dante was a career soldier, a man of dark, curling hair and dark brow, not quick to trust anyone, incapable of believing anything good of Zor.

The sergeant grabbed Zor's leather torso harness and gave it a yank, nearly lifting him off his feet. "What about it?"

Zor shook his head slowly, as if coming out of a trance. "Angie! Wh—how did I get here?" He blinked, looking around him.

"That's my line. You're sneakin' around a restricted area and you're away from your duty station without permission. If you don't have a pretty good explanation, I'm gonna see to it your butt goes into Barbwire City for a long time!" He shook Zor again.

"Oh, Zor! There you are!" First Lieutenant Dana Sterling, commanding officer of the 15th, practically squealed it as she rounded a corner and hurried toward them. Angelo shook his head a little, watching how her smile beamed and her eyes crinkled as she caught sight of Zor.

Like her two subordinates, she was dressed in the white Southern Cross uniform, with the black piping and black boots that suggested a riding outfit. She barely reached the middle of Angelo's chest, but she was, he had to admit, a gutsy and capable officer. Except where this Zor guy was concerned.

She rushed up to them and grabbed Zor's hand; Angelo found himself automatically releasing his captive. Dana seemed completely unaware that she had blundered into the middle of what would otherwise have been a fight. "I've been looking for you *everywhere*, Zor!"

Zor, still dazed, seemed to be groping for words. "Just a second, Lieutenant," Angelo interrupted.

But she was tugging Zor away. "Come along; I want to ask you something!"

"Hold it, ma'am!" Angelo burst out. "Why don'tcha ask pretty boy here, what he's doing hanging around a restricted area?"

Dana's expression turned to anger. Like the sergeant, she had tracked down Zor with difficulty, but she wouldn't let herself think badly of her strange, alien trooper. She shot back, "What are you, Angie, a spy for the Global Military Police?"

Angelo's black brows went up. "Huh? You know better than that! But somebody has to keep an eye on this guy. Or don't you think what he's doing is a little suspicious?"

Dana rasped, "Zor's suffering from severe memory loss. If he's a little disoriented at times, that just means we should show him a bit of compassion and understanding!"

She slipped an arm through Zor's, clasping his elbow. Angelo wondered if he were going crazy; wasn't this the same alien who had led the enemy forces in his red Bioroid? Didn't he try to kill Dana, as she had tried to kill him, in a half dozen or so of the most vicious single combats of the war, her Hovertank mecha against his Bioroid?

"I'll speak to you later, Sergeant," Dana said, dragging Zor off.

Angelo watched them go. He had gained a lot of respect for Dana Sterling since she had taken command of the 15th, but she was only eighteen and, in the sergeant's opinion, still too impulsive and too inclined to make rash moves. He tried to suppress his sneaking suspicion as to why she was so protective of Zor—so possessive, really.

But one indisputable fact remained. No matter how loyally Angelo tried to discount it, Dana herself was half alien . . .

ABOUT THE AUTHOR

Jack McKinney has been a psychiatric aide, fusion-rock guitarist and session man, worldwide wilderness guide, and "consultant" to the U.S. Military in Southeast Asia (although they had to draft him for that).

His numerous other works of mainstream and science fiction—novels, radio and television scripts—have been written under various pseudonyms.

He currently resides in Dos Lagunas, El Petén, Guatemala.